27777.

G

TH

THE REVOLUTIONARY'S DAUGHTER

The Revolutionary's Daughter

Gwen Grant

MAMMOTH

First published in Great Britain 1990
by William Heinemann Ltd
Published 1991 by Mammoth
an imprint of Mandarin Paperbacks
Michelin House, 81 Fulham Road, London SW3 6RB

Mandarin is an imprint of the Octopus Publishing Group,
a division of Reed International Books Ltd

ISBN 0 7497 0422 5

A CIP catalogue record for this title
is available from the British Library

Printed in Great Britain
by Cox & Wyman Ltd, Reading, Berkshire

Chapter One

When she looked back, Violette could almost name the minute her mother decided to leave them; still feel the fear she had felt when Janis had looked first at the television and then at her, at Mark, at their father.

'I don't believe this,' her mother had shouted. 'I just don't believe it.'

They had all stared at the bright screen. Violette could hear Janis's voice, panic and outrage spilling over as they watched the convoys of police vans speeding up the motorways, dominating the roads of the country and all, every last van it seemed, heading for their home area. For their people.

That had been the start. March 1984 and the Miners' Strike began to take on new and terrifying dimensions.

'There can never be any justification for this.' Janis choked on angry tears. 'Never. No reason could be strong enough for this . . . this bloody charade.'

'I don't know what you're getting so upset about,' Violette's Dad said idly. 'This is nothing to do with you. It's not your fight. Let them sort it out between them, that's what I say.'

He smiled a sharp irritated smile at his wife.

Violette saw the flare of answering irritation in her mother's face. The way her lips tightened so that tiny lines showed on the fair skin.

Well, you *would* say that, wouldn't you, Peter?' she returned. 'I wouldn't expect *you* to say anything else. In fact, I'd be very surprised if you did say anything else.'

'Here we go again,' Mark muttered.

'Oh, shut up, Mark.'

Violette frowned at her brother, afraid Janis would leap to her feet and vanish into the kitchen. Too many evenings lately that had happened. Her mother in the kitchen, her Dad morose and silent. It was horrible in the house then.

'I'm going to make a cup of tea,' Janis said. 'How you can just sit there like that defeats me.'

She eyed her husband with impatient scorn and repeated, 'Not as I expect anything else from you.'

Peter leapt to his feet and flung the newspaper on the floor.

'Why don't you lay off? What do you want me to do? Man the barricades?' He laughed. 'You're the same as them all, aren't you? Send somebody else out to do your dirty work.'

That was the moment for Violette. It was then she thought her mother had decided she would leave. But nothing happened immediately.

The weeks went by until that beautiful April Saturday, clear and sunny, when the miners poured into the town from all over the area. The police almost outnumbered the miners. They gathered in the surrounding streets of the town, on horseback, on foot, in cars, and in the now familiar dark vans. Smaller numbers mingled with the Miners' Parade. The rest waited.

The pit men marched down the town's main street as if they were on holiday, as if they were unaware of the huge police presence. They carried banners which bellied out in the stiff little wind.

Women and children joined with the men. This was something new. This hadn't been seen before, women and children walking beside the men of their families.

'You could be in an Iron Curtain country,' Janis said as she watched them, still cheerful, still being British to their bootlaces.

The prams and pushchairs were full of babies with ice-cream cornets and dancing flags.

'Flags!' Janis could hardly bear it. 'Flags. They might as well carry shrouds.'

Violette glanced at her.

'Why do you have to take everything so personally?' she complained. 'What's it to you what they're carrying?'

It was so gay and colourful. There was the living quilt of colours as the procession wound past, with a startling sudden black of clergy, a gold cross banging the sunshine back into the street.

There were the big Union banners worked with tapestry lions and old-fashioned steadfast faces. She wondered what those dead men would have made of the strike.

For weeks it went on, with terrible scenes all over the country. Scenes of horror and shame. Mounted police charging men and women, leaning from their saddles and smacking out with their long-handled truncheons.

Violette found it impossible to believe that these police were the same as the policemen who came into school and talked about their work, encouraging the children to treat them as reliable friends.

She remembered when they'd had the accident in the car. Those policemen had been kind and reassuring. Who were these new men?

There were police everywhere and Violette's mother grew more and more angry.

'Do you see they don't have numbers on their uniforms?

Do you see that?'

Often, when they went out, the police stopped the car and searched it. Some days they stopped and searched it when they went out, stopped and searched it when they came back.

'What are you looking for?' Janis asked them.

They never answered. She answered herself.

'They're looking for miners,' she would say. 'Miners two foot tall. Here –' she'd point. 'You've missed a bit. I might have one under the floor carpet.'

'Mum,' Violette would mumur. 'Give over.'

'Give over! Give over! Where are we? Go on, tell me, where are we? Poland? Russia? My God, I don't believe this.'

Slowly, people's perception of the police changed with the change in the police themselves. Not only did these men not answer but it began to appear they were answerable to no-one.

Violette dreaded the confrontation between Janis and the police.

'Oh, Mum,' she groaned, when they started. 'Please be quiet. They'll arrest you.'

'They want to arrest me. Just let them. I'd show them, all right. I'd soon show them what happens when they arrest innocent people.'

Violette squirmed in the car seat. She wished she'd never come out with her mother. It was the same every time. Janis seemed to delight in confrontations, in shouting, and yet, yet, she could see her mother's hands shaking. She could tell Janis was frightened, so why did she act the way she did?

'You wouldn't know what to do,' she flared from her own fear. 'If they took you away. If they pushed you into one of those vans. You wouldn't know what to do at all.'

They both stared at the darkened van windows, and Violette felt her mother shudder.

'No,' she said. 'You're right. I wouldn't know what to do but there's plenty of women would. We're learning all the time, women are. We have to learn before it's too late.'

Violette thought of the women. The women pouring into their house at night, in the afternoon, at weekends. Anne, Joan, Pat, Sandra, Sharon, Becky, Maureen. She'd lost count of their names. There were so many of them. They changed from group to group.

They were the ones who had put her mother up to all this. She knew they were. When the women were there, her mother did nothing but talk. Talk and smoke and drink coffee.

They were nothing like the quiet soft-spoken women Violette had once known who had come to her mother's door. These were noisy women. Rowdy. They shouted a lot. Laughed. Made plans. Read books. Wrote speeches. Made speeches. Wept. Grew silent and tired. Fell asleep. Wore red lips on white faces. Seemed to live more inside themselves than outside.

They tried to talk to her. One after the other.

'Your mother's waking up to things,' Joan said once. 'So should you. You should be aware. There are no fights left that women can just leave to men. We're all in the same boat and the boat's leaking. Sinking. Ignorance is no excuse any more, Violette. No woman can afford to be ignorant. You should listen and learn, my girl, while you've got the chance. Before anything else takes you unawares.'

'What makes you think I haven't listened?' Violette retorted sharply. 'It never seems to occur to you, does it, that I might not like what I hear. That I might not care.'

The buzz of noise in the room had quietened so that her words fell into the middle of the silence.

'I don't see why I should have you lot in my life,' the girl went on. 'You were even here at my sixteenth birthday and I didn't invite you. I never asked you to come.'

'That'll do,' her mother said, appearing at her side.

'It's all right for you,' the girl shouted. 'You seem to think you can do what you want with my life as well as your own. Well, you can't. It's my life and it belongs to me.'

Violette turned and stormed up to her room, pacing up and down for hours until the house was quiet. As soon as she heard the door close behind the last person, she hurried down, wanting to tackle Janis, wanting a blazing row – but she found the rooms empty.

The women had gone and her mother had gone with them. There was a note on the table. 'Gone to a meeting. Back soon. Mum.'

Staring at the piece of paper, Violette had felt that marked the real beginning of change. Her mother leaving, without even shouting up the stairs. Not bothering to let her know when she'd be back.

More and more police flooded into the small town. They were everywhere, walking about in pairs. No-one asked the time or the way any more. People grew guarded in the face of these strangers.

There were bitter, noisy vigils. Families were split down the middle as some men returned to work, others stayed out. Mothers and fathers grieved over children taking different paths and women stood solidly by their men.

In the middle of the marches, the protests, the demonstrations, Violette's mother now took her place.

Violette would not go with her.

'I don't want to go and I don't want you to go. You've no right to be there. It's nothing to do with you. Why are you doing it?'

Janis refused to answer. She had tried explanation. All

10

that brought was trouble. Now she just shrugged her shoulders.

Sometimes it seemed to Violette that none of it was real.

Then, her father finally snapped.

'You're really enjoying this, Janis, aren't you?' he demanded. 'Thrown yourself into it, you and your friends.'

Janis grew still and watchful.

'You're just making a nonsense out of it all,' he went on. 'Do you know what you're doing? What you're marching for? Fighting for? Eh? Eh? You've never given politics a second thought before, so why now? You make me laugh with your protests. I tell you one thing. They're not worth the sound of them. Not worth one blind thing.'

Violette noticed how tired he was under the anger. There were blue smudges under his eyes. His mouth was tight with strain. His hands were edgy, knuckling up, straightening out, brushing, touching, scratching, rubbing.

'At least I *do* something,' Janis threw back but her husband wouldn't have it.

'I do something, too. I hold my end up. I support what I believe in. Do you think you've got a monopoly on feelings? Have you looked at this house lately? Have you seen the state of this house?'

Mark jumped to his feet, scattering his school papers over the carpet. He stood in front of them with fists clenched, his face paper white.

'Why don't you shut up? Shut up. Shut up! You're always rowing. Always shouting,' and then the boy flung himself out of the room and Violette heard his feet thundering on the stairs.

'He'll get a sick headache now and then he'll be moaning and groaning all night being ill.'

She looked at her mother.

'Don't you care?'

11

'Of course I care.'

'*I* don't think you do. I think the only thing you care about is those women. It's your fault, all this. Why don't you keep away from them? Why don't you behave like you used to?' And then, finally, on a wail she couldn't do anything about, 'Why have you changed?'

Janis seemed almost to stop breathing. She looked round the room as if it was all new to her and she had no part, no place in it.

'Go and see to your brother,' she said at last. 'Go on. Don't argue.'

Resentfully, Violette trailed out and up to Mark's room, but even when she knocked he wouldn't answer, wouldn't open the door to her.

'Come on, Mark,' she tried. 'Open the door.'

Then he did shout out.

'You go away!'

She could hear the cracks in his voice.

'No. Don't send me away.' She tried again. 'Open the door.'

'I don't want to talk to you. I don't want to talk to anybody. You're as bad as they are. I'm fed up with this rotten house. Fed up. Go away. Just leave me alone.'

Violette leant against the door jamb. It seemed everybody wanted to be left alone. She turned to go back down the stairs but then Mark's door swung open.

He stood in front of her, head bent, hands clenched at his sides.

'I hate them,' he said. 'Oh, I hate them.'

Violette put her arms round him.

'I know.'

They stood together a few moments, sharing their distress.

'OK now?' she asked and when he nodded, left him,

closing the door quietly behind her.

When she walked back into the room downstairs, she knew with solid certainty that things had grown worse between her mother and father. They were standing, heads turned from each other and the silence in the room was so electric, Violette felt a sudden move would be fatal.

'You've had your say, Peter,' her mother exploded.

'And you've had yours.'

'But mine isn't quite complete.' Janis's face was bleak. 'I can't stay with you after what you've said . . . accused me of. I've no option. There's nothing else for me to do. I have to go.'

'Go?' Violette's father repeated stupidly. 'Go where?'

'Anywhere. Anywhere away from here.'

Violette was frightened.

'You can't go away, Mum. Please don't go away.'

Her mother turned to her.

'Violette –' she began. 'Sometimes you have to do things . . .'

'Don't start that rubbish,' her husband butted in. 'You don't have to do anything. You're going because you want to. This is the way you've planned it from the beginning. This strike has given you exactly what you wanted. You've used it, Janis, used it to get your own way. Just like everybody else.'

Her mother paled.

'I have *not* used it!' she denied. 'I have not used it. It isn't like that at all. It's . . . it's opened my eyes to what's happening in my own life. That's what it's done and I can't undo that, not even if I wanted to. I don't know why you're so bothered, anyway. You put the house before me. "Have you seen the state of this house?"' she mimicked. 'As if the house mattered. As if it's a living thing. As if it could live and walk and talk and breathe. *I* can do those things. The house can't. And it's your house as well as mine. You wouldn't mortify me if you did the cleaning.'

'I do my share.'

'But I don't think your share is a big enough share.'

'Mum.'

'Be quiet, Violette.' Janis was almost crying. 'I can tell you one thing, Peter. I hate what's been happening. You – getting on at me all the time. Violette – not even trying to understand. Mark –'

'For God's sake,' he interrupted. 'What's wrong with you? Me, Violette, Mark. Mark isn't old enough to tell the time of day. It's you. Go on, go through us all. Don't forget to blame the cat, and the budgie –' he laughed without humour. 'And there's the goldfish – what did that do wrong? It must have done something. Swum round its bowl the wrong way, I expect. Everybody must understand Janis because nobody understands her, nobody, and Janis is too busy to understand anyone herself.'

Violette found she was shaking. She tried to speak but her mother's face was brilliant with rage and when Violette finally managed half a word, those snapping eyes turned on her and made her tongue-tied and afraid.

'Don't row,' she begged. 'Please don't row.'

Her mother turned to the door, hurrying through it. They heard her quick footsteps across the hall. The tap of her hand on the banister as she hurried upstairs.

What happened next seemed like part of a dark dream. In minutes Janis was back in the room flinging a bag on the sofa.

'I'm leaving,' she said. 'And I won't take one single thing of yours with me. Not one thing. You . . . you –' she pleated her lips together and Violette could see now the angry tears pouring down her face.

'Oh, God,' her mother called. 'Just let me be free.'

Later, Violette could bring the whole ugly scene back in every detail. It haunted her nights and stalked her days and she thought that she would never forget it, not as long as she lived.

Chapter Two

The thing that Violette found most confusing was that
no-one tried to stop her mother.

She felt she herself should have taken matters into her
own hands and should have moved forward, perhaps
slapped Janis across the face. That would have stopped
her. Violette had to grin unwillingly as she thought of what
would have happened if she'd tried that. Her mother
would have retaliated – and how.

But – her face darkened – her Dad hadn't made a move
towards his wife. When he finally seemed to come to his
senses, it was only in the most half hearted way that he
called 'Stop it.' His eyes flicked to his daughter. He was
shocked by her pale face and his voice grew louder, firmer.

'I said stop it.'

Janis ignored him.

First, she took off her blouse. She folded it neatly before
laying it on the table. Next, her skirt. Once the heavy
material was free from her legs, she seemed to take heart,
grow lighter. To Violette her mother seemed airier. A
sense of release started to creep into the room.

Then Janis kicked off her small brown shoes. The
chestnutty leather gleamed, for Violette's father polished
all the shoes, every morning. It was part of his pride. 'With
clean shoes, no-one can tell if you're rich or poor,' he

would say.

'Mum —' Violette jerked forward, as if she were on a string. 'Please, Mum, stop it.'

Her mother stared through her as if she didn't exist. As if her body didn't take up any space or light or air.

'Pass me that bag,' Janis demanded, not looking at anyone.

Violette looked round to where the bag lay so innocently on the sofa. She reached for it as if it were a bomb. Picking it up, she held it out to her mother. For a moment, she hated Janis with such force, she felt she might actually crash the bag into her.

Her father inclined his head.

'Go and wait in the next room,' he said but Janis stopped her.

'You needn't worry. I'm not taking anything else off.'

Janis emptied the bag on the floor. A black skirt fell out. Black shoes. A black cardigan. Jacket.

Violette watched her mother put these clothes on. She watched the narrow feet slide into the shoes. Blouse. Skirt. Cardigan. Watched her mother drag a comb through her hair and disarrange the blonde curls, twisting the fall of hair then snapping an elastic band round it.

Her husband turned and saw her.

'Mother Russia, I presume,' he said and Violette saw the little smile in his eyes. She smiled too in the warmth of a family joke but Janis didn't find it funny.

'Oh, go on. Laugh at me. You always have done so why change now?'

'You can't be serious about this?' he pointed to the clothes. 'I mean, my God, Janis, you can't expect me to take that seriously.'

'You look horrible,' Violette muttered and found she was trembling so much she could hardly get the words out.

17

'Well,' Janis said. 'I certainly get a vote of confidence around here.'

There was an uncomfortable silence.

'Do you see me, Peter?' Janis asked. 'Do you see me? Not your wife. Not your children's mother – but me. Me. Do you see now what I am?'

Violette had a feeling things could have changed at that point but it was gone in an instant as her Dad returned, 'See you? Oh, yes, I see you, all right. I've seen enough today to last me for a lifetime.'

Violette started to cry. She hadn't meant to but she couldn't get hold of why this was happening. Why should it happen to them? To her? To her Mum and Dad and Mark?

'Well, you won't see me any more because I'm leaving. I'm leaving this house, this way of life, you, and I'm going to start being myself. I'm going to –'

'But what about us?' Violette cried. 'What are we going to do without you?'

She felt faint with pain.

Her mother shrugged.

'You're old enough to cope now, Violette, and I shall still be around. I have no intention of leaving you and Mark for ever, without seeing you again. You're part of me – how could I leave you both and not see you any more? Don't worry. I'll be in touch as soon as I've settled.'

Violette rubbed at the tears on her cheeks.

'Don't let us keep you then,' Peter snapped. 'I'm sure we don't want to be responsible for holding you back from your quest for truth. We wouldn't want to keep you here, stunting your growth. Asking you to be a normal woman, a normal wife and mother. God forbid that we should ask that of you, Janis.'

'Stop it!' Violette screamed so that she frightened

herself. 'Mum, please, take those horrible things off and stay here with us.'

'Stay here? Stay with that man and this life? I'd die first.'

'I'll make you a cup of coffee. You'll feel better then. Honest, you'll feel much better after a cup of coffee. Let me make one for you. It'll only take me a minute.'

Her mother shook her head and went across to the girl. She put her arms round her and for a brief moment, held her close. Violette could hardly breathe for the smell of the clothes. The material seemed clogged with old perfume and face powder.

'Don't cry, love.'

She pulled out of her mother's arms.

'Those things aren't your clothes. They don't belong to you. You don't know who's worn them. It's disgusting. Why don't you take them off?'

Her mother looked down at the black clothing.

'Don't be silly, Violette. There's nothing wrong with these clothes. They're perfectly clean. Anyway, I shall take them off when I get some new.' She was impatient, as if she were tired of the whole business. 'You don't think I'd stay in these any longer than I have to, do you? They're just rehearsal clothes. For a play I'm in. That's all.'

'What was that, then? A trial run?' her husband asked. 'A rehearsal, was it, for the real thing? Do you leave your husband and children in that play as well?'

'You can't act,' Violette accused.

'I've acted for the last fifteen years of my life. There can't be much else to learn.'

'Why don't you just go?'

Peter jerked his arm.

'Go on. Just go and let's get this over and done with.'

Janis turned away from them. They stood, Violette and her father, watching her pick up her handbag and tip it onto the table. Watched her sort out her credit card, allowance books, gold compact, lipstick, and then her hand hovered over the cards. 'Take them,' Peter said but Janis pushed them away.

'No. No, I'll manage.'

'Please yourself.'

He picked up the plastic cards and snapped them in two.

The loud retorts of the breaking plastic made all their nerves jump.

She took a pack of cigarettes, a box of matches and some pound coins. Stuffing them in her pocket, she hesitated and then looked at her daughter.

'I'm sorry. Honestly, I'm sorry.'

Violette watched in stunned disbelief as her mother's slim body moved across the room. Janis stopped at the door.

'Tell Mark I'll be in touch.'

She did not look back.

Then she was gone. The door slammed behind her.

The noise echoed in the house and Violette thought the closing door sounded not an ending but a beginning of pain and loneliness for them all.

'That's that, then,' her Dad said and she saw his set face tighten as he scooped up Janis's clothing. 'The sooner we get back to normal, the better.'

Violette felt as if she had turned into a block of ice. She couldn't persuade her feet to move or her mouth to open.

Her Dad hustled her through to the kitchen.

'Come on. Come on,' he chivvied her along, worried about the dull sick look she had. 'You put the kettle on.'

She watched through the kitchen window as he marched down the yard and tore the lid off the bin. She felt herself almost drowning as he stuffed the skirt and shoes into the bin liner. Then the blouse. He slammed the lid on and turned away.

She held the kettle under the tap until the water poured everywhere.

'Behind you,' she whispered but she could hardly hear herself, even though she was sure she was screaming. 'Behind you,' she tried again.

Her Dad came back into the room, bringing the night air with him and Violette stared at him as if he were a stranger.

'The bin,' she mumbled and then, pushing him to one side, ran down the path to the bin.

One long pink sleeve was trapped by the rubber lid. It flopped down the side of the bin as if it were appealing for help. She could see her mother caught in the blackness, shut off, packed away, only that pink sleeve a reminder of what had been, as if it were waving for help.

She pulled at the sleeve, crying. She couldn't release it. 'Oh. Oh.'

Dimly she heard the moaning.

She had a vivid picture of her mother in the bin, thrown away. Dead.

'She's caught. Caught,' she cried again and again until her father hurried back down to her.

He lifted the bin lid and pulled the blouse out. Violette held it. The cold slippery material slid through her fingers and, in a sudden revulsion of feeling, she had torn the blouse and pushed it deep into the plastic bag.

Her father put the lid back on. There was such sorrow in the air. They walked back down the path to the kitchen. This time when Violette filled the kettle, she did it properly and snapped the window blind shut without another glance down the garden.

With studied determination, her father tried to keep things normal. He insisted she have her supper. Insisted on taking Mark the same. He put out biscuits and she nibbled at one, pretending she was eating it and was hungry.

Mark devoured biscuits and tea and came down, asking if he could have toast. He burnt the bread, wandering back upstairs scattering black crumbs behind him.

At last, in the end, Violette's Dad put his coat on.

'I'm going for a pint. Don't wait up. I shan't be long.' And then he too was gone.

Drearily, Violette tidied up. She wandered through the silent house.

Everywhere she went, she could smell her mother. See her mother. The brush in the bathroom was full of blonde hairs. The dressing table had her mother's silver backed brush on it. Her mother's books and papers and magazines were all over. Her plants, her shoes, her hasty flowers in vases, her talcum powder, perfume, hair spray, everywhere.

Janis was in the house in all but body.

As it grew later and darker, Mark reappeared. He padded through the rooms and switched lights on.

'What are you sitting in the dark for?' he grumbled. 'Scare anybody half to death. I'm hungry again. Is there anything on TV? What time is it?' He barely waited for an answer before rushing on, 'Where's Mum?'

'She's gone.'

'Where has she gone?'

Violette shrugged.

'I dunno. I don't know where she's gone.'

The boy persisted.

'Is she coming back?'

'I shouldn't think so. She didn't seem to me as if she would come back.'

Mark looked out of the window at the familiar street.

'I'm hungry. I never had any dinner. Isn't there anything

proper to eat?'

Violette was tired but she forced herself to her feet and went to look in the fridge and the cupboards. She found a frozen meat pie, a can of potatoes, beans.

She banged them down on the table.

'You can cook these if you want,' she said and Mark picked up the pie and read every single word of the instructions, three times, out loud.

At last, angry, Violette took the food and started to prepare it.

'Time you learnt to do things for yourself,' she said with weary impatience. 'You can be your own skivvy from now on, I'm not going to be it. You'll have to learn, Mark.'

'Why don't you just shut up,' the boy fired. 'I'll do them. Leave them. Leave them alone. You're always moaning, you are. Just leave them and I'll do them myself.'

He stormed about the kitchen, dragging the pie out of her hands, slamming the beans on, pouring the potatoes into a pan.

'Anybody'd think you were cooking a feast.'

In the middle of it all, their Dad wandered in. The smell of beer cancelled out the other smells.

'What have you got in the oven?' he asked.

Mark grumbled.

'A pie. Don't ask her –' he jerked his head – 'to do anything for you. It's more trouble than it's worth.'

'I think I fancy a piece of pie.'

Peter sat down. He felt worn out.

'You go and watch TV, Dad,' Violette said. 'I'll do this.'

Mark grinned.

'Will you do mine as well?'

She nodded.

She heard the click of the television and then music filled the house.

Standing there, seeing her mother undress again and again, Violette got an inkling of what might be coming her way.

She kicked the pantry door.

'Wherever are you, mother. Wherever you are, I hate you.'

Chapter Three

The weeks crawled past. Violette could never remember time being so long. There seemed to be so much of it. She would get up, go to school, come home, prepare a meal and throw her homework on the floor.

'Have you done your homework?' her father would ask, staring at the television screen.

Violette would say 'Yes' or 'No' as the fancy took her but whatever she said, her father simply nodded and murmured, 'That's good.'

He went away for a couple of days and the first morning he was away, Violette woke to the smell of frying bacon. She lay in bed, sniffing the lovely smell of bread toasting, listening to the small sounds of breakfast being prepared.

Then, she realised what was happening and sat bolt upright. In seconds, she was on her feet and out into the top hall. Mark appeared beside her.

'Has she come back?' he asked. 'Do you think it's her down there?'

They took the stairs two at a time and went crashing into the kitchen.

Their Granny looked up in surprise as they burst through the door.

'Why,' she said, 'I didn't expect this. Your dad said you never got up till the last minute. Still,' she went on briskly, ignoring their stricken faces, 'now you're up, you can stay up. Go on, the pair of you. Get yourselves washed and then come down for your breakfast.'

They trailed back upstairs. Violette had tried to say something but the words wouldn't come. She had only been reminded once again how strong the likeness was between her mother and her granny. They seemed to have been made out of the same piece of bone. Violette was like her father. Tall, where they were small. Dark, where they were fair.

Neither speaking, they got ready for school. Mark was in and out of the bathroom in minutes and Violette barely washed her face. She noticed her fingernails were edged with dirt but she couldn't be bothered to clean them. She dragged a comb through her hair and went sullenly down to the kitchen.

'You can just go back and get a shower, Mark,' her gran was saying. 'I've never seen ears like yours since . . . well, since I don't know when and that's the truth. Go on. Back. Back.' And she hustled the unwilling boy out of the room.

Violette reached for a piece of toast and her Granny pounced.

'As for you, I'm surprised at you. Have you looked in a mirror lately?'

Violette flushed but refused to answer. Her Granny snatched the food out of her hand.

'You're getting no breakfast until you've cleaned those nails. And put some clean clothes on and seen to your face. It's dirty. As for your hair . . .'

'I don't want any breakfast.' Violette sprang up, sending the chair crashing behind her. 'You can keep your rotten old breakfast.'

Her Granny moved fast across the kitchen and took the girl by the hand. She dragged Violette back up the stairs, and, shouting and bellowing at each other, they went banging into the bathroom.

Mark ducked behind the shower curtain.

'Here! Can't you get any privacy in this house?'

Violette grabbed a handful of the shiny plastic, trying to dig her heels in. Without warning, the whole curtain fell over the woman and the girl, the wet plastic clinging to their heads and faces.

'What the –' Violette heard her Granny exclaim. 'Where are you, Violette? My life, I never knew anything like this.' The cross voice went on and on, grumbling and spluttering. 'For goodness' sake, get me out of here.'

The small bathroom was choked with bodies.

Then, the plastic sheet pulled away and Mark's furious face glared down at them.

'Blinking messing about. I'm in here, trying to get a shower, if you don't mind. You'd think I didn't blinking exist, I'm not kidding.'

His towel slipped and, hastily, the boy grabbed it round him.

Violette started to giggle. Her grandmother's pink, startled face turned towards her.

'You should see your hair,' Violette laughed.

'You should see your own,' her Granny retorted.

'I can feel it,' Violette bubbled with laughter. 'And your face, Gran,' she shrieked. 'You should see your face. What a surprise you got.'

The girl roared. She couldn't help it. The more she looked at Mark and her Granny, the funnier it all seemed.

Her Granny smiled, then, 'Do stop it, Violette.'

Mark, angrier than ever, knotted the towel round his waist and tried, with futile dignity, to restore the shower curtain to its normal place.

'I'll leave you to get yourself clean,' her Granny said now

and Violette nodded, all laughter gone in an instant.

Later, after breakfast, her Granny said, 'You know your Mum's with us, don't you?'

Violette nodded.

'You should come and see her. She misses you.'

'Why should I come and see her?' the girl said tensely. 'Why should I have anything to do with her at all?'

'She is your mother.'

'I know that. You know that. The only person who doesn't know it is her. She doesn't want to be my mother. She just wants to do her own thing.'

Her Granny moved some pots out of the way.

'I know for a fact she's tried to see you every day for a fortnight. You're never in. At least, that's what your Dad says.'

Violette groaned.

'She doesn't want to see me,' she said. 'She just wants to . . . to . . .' she stopped, unable to put what she felt into words.

'Hmmmm. Let me ask you something,' her Granny started. 'If I said to you "What do you want to be when you leave school?" what would you say?'

The girl kicked the base of the kitchen table, refusing to answer, refusing to look at her Gran.

'Come on, answer me. What would you say?'

'I don't know.'

'Well, I daresay you wouldn't say you just wanted to be a mother, would you?'

'Would you?' she persisted. 'Your mother was always a strong-minded girl, Violette. She always did everything with all her heart. When she met your Dad, nothing would do but that they should be married. No –' she held up a quietening hand. 'I'm not saying anything against your Dad. He's a good man and he's been good to Janis. All I'm saying is your mother would never have said she just wanted to have children and bring them up and . . . all that.'

'Then she shouldn't have *had* us, should she?'

'She had you over sixteen years ago,' her Granny snapped, then sighed, then sat down. 'Forget it. Forget it. But listen, just this one last thing. Have you ever wondered where your name came from?'

Violette looked at her in surprise.

'No.'

'It seems to me you don't think at all, my girl.' Then, 'No, no, let's start again. This name of yours has a special meaning for your mother.' She sighed, paused, then went on. 'You were named after a war heroine. A girl called Violette Szabo. She died, of course, died for what she believed in. There were millions of young people died for what they believed in.'

Violette tried to imagine this other Violette.

'I don't know why Violette Szabo's story caught your mother's imagination the way it did. All I know is that it did. She was really fired by it. She read everything she could about her. A film was made and your Mum didn't give us a minute's peace until we took her to see it. It wasn't on here. It was being shown about twelve miles away and she pestered me and your Grandad until we finally agreed to take her. She wouldn't let us go in with her, though. She said she wanted to see it on her own and she did. She came out –' She sighed again. 'I don't know. She came out of that cinema almost . . . almost radiant. I've never seen anyone so affected by a film.'

Violette shrugged.

'All I'm saying is . . . try and understand that your mum used to be a girl once. Same hopes, same dreams. Sometimes the dreams don't die, that's all. Sometimes they live on as long as life itself.'

'I don't dream of being a war heroine. Is that what all this is about, then?' She banged her toe into the back of a chair. 'Her wanting to be a heroine?'

Her Granny rose to her feet.

'I think I've wasted my time. I don't think we ought to talk about it any more.'

'Well, that suits me. It suits me fine. I can't see this has got anything to do with anything. So, OK, she had a crush on a war heroine but that was her crush, not mine. And I'll bet you one thing. I'll bet this other Violette's Mum didn't leave her.'

'No. She left her mother.'

'Isn't that the way it's supposed to be? That other Violette, she died knowing her and her Mum were on the same side, didn't she? Not like me and my Mum. We're not on the same side. She's on her side and I'm on mine and I don't even know what side mine is.'

There was nothing more to say. They tidied up in silence, set the table ready for the evening meal and left together.

Violette watched her Granny walk away. She didn't look old. She walked very loosely and she was still pretty. Looking at her Granny was almost like looking at her mother in years to come.

She wandered to school. Mark caught up with her. They walked along, both deep in their own thoughts, scarcely aware of each other.

Because Violette was staring, unseeing, at the ground, she didn't notice the group of girls standing at the side of the pavement, dragging blossom out of a tree and pinning it in their hair.

'Hello, slag.'

That was the first Violette knew of their presence.

'I said "Hello, slag".' The voice rang hard in the soft air. Violette stopped, trying to bring things into focus.

'I think she means you,' Mark said, nudging her arm.

Violette looked at Rachel Benton. Her continued silence seemed to madden the girl.

'What's up, gormless?' Rachel asked.

Now Violette was only too aware of the group of girls. They stood around Rachel in a solid little phalanx, grinning their spiteful smiles, slyness running in and out of their faces.

'Reckon cat's got her tongue, Rache,' they sneered.

'It's only what you'd expect of a slag,' Rachel Benton said. 'Her – and her mother.'

Violette stiffened.

'What do you mean? What are you talking about?'

'Ha! So you have got a tongue. What am I talking about? I'll tell you what I'm talking about, slag. I'm talking about your mother, standing outside Burton's every night, collecting with a tin can, that's what I'm talking about. They gave her a tin of beans, you know,' she went on, her voice brittle with spite. 'They gave her a tin of beans and she said "Ho, thenk yew very much."' She stressed the words again. '"Thenk yew very much."'

'I don't know what you're talking about.'

Rachel caught hold of Violette's coat. She tried to pull her close but, to her own surprise, Violette resisted and the other girl stumbled.

'Take your hands off me, Benton.'

'Oh. Miss High and Mighty, I am sure.' The girl paused. 'Don't you want to know why your mother's a slag, slag?'

Violette knocked the girl's arm away with a fury that shocked them both.

Benton wet her lips.

'Don't you call me a slag. And don't call my mother one, either.'

'I shall call you what I want. Who's to stop me?'

'Go on. You tell her, Rache,' the crowd of girls chanted. 'You give her what for.'

Violette didn't even glance at them. All at once, she felt a murderous rage. A fury so intense and deep that she started to shake.

Rachel took a step closer.

'She's a slag, your mother is. Always knew she was, when she thought she was a cut above everybody else. Just like you, Miss High and Mighty. Well, you've been brought down now, haven't you?'

Without a word, Violette hit the sneering face in front of her. Blood spurted from the girl's nose. There was a shocked silence. Rachel lifted a hand to her face and when it came down stained in her own blood, she grabbed Violette's hair and smeared the blood over the girl's face.

Then, they were fighting. Violette had never thought she could fight. Had never wanted to fight. Now, they fought. The crowd shouted and yelled, calling for Rachel.

Mark wondered if he should intervene. He stood, indecisive.

The shrill voices rising, falling, then rising again didn't matter to Violette. All she could feel was this rage.

They fell in the end, crashing to the ground. The two girls rolled in the wide sweeps and drifts of pale flowers that had dropped from the trees.

Violette could hear Rachel grunting. It was an odd ugly sound, the breath exploding from the girl's mouth.

Then, a blow caught her eye and Violette became aware of pain.

Their audience had stopped shouting, silenced by the intensity of the fight. They stood, uneasy, as Rachel and

Violette rolled off the grass into the road. The car that was almost on them braked fiercely. The smell of burning rubber filled the air.

The two girls suddenly found themselves hauled to their feet.

'What on earth do you two think you're doing?' the voice roared. 'I've never seen such an exhibition. How old are you?' He shook them. 'How old are you? Two? Three?'

They were stunned by the anger.

'I swear I don't know what gets into you girls,' Mr Davies shouted. 'Thirty years I've been teaching at this school and never, never,' he roared, 'have I seen anything like this. Rolling into the road, under innocent people's cars.' He shook them again. 'All right, all right. Just tell me, what kind of impression does this make of the school?'

He let them go and they faced him like small children.

'You –' he prodded Rachel. 'You tell me.'

Rachel didn't answer.

'You, then.' He turned to Violette.

Violette was silent.

'Look, you two. Look around you. Can you see everybody staring? Can you? Can you?'

'Don't you touch me.' Rachel lifted her hand.

The teacher ignored her. 'This is going to look good, isn't it?' he snapped. 'Fighting like this. Common fighting, that's what this is. Common fighting by common girls.'

Both girls frowned at this.

Mr Davies grew calmer. He leant against his car, shaken by the near miss.

'I don't expect it of you, Violette. What's got into you? And you, Rachel. I thought you'd left this kind of behaviour behind.'

Rachel sniggered.

'Don't laugh at me, girl.' He turned to Violette. 'Wait till your parents hear about this.'

'She hasn't got no parents. Her mother's on the streets. She's a slag, her mother is.'

Mr Davies restrained Violette.

'That'll do, Miss Benton. Now, I'm going to let you both go and I swear, if either of you touch the other, I'll keep you in detention till Christmas. Right?'

They both nodded.

'Right. You lot –' he shouted at the crowd of gaping girls. 'Get on up to school.' Seeing Mark, he went on, 'What's wrong with you, Saunders? Why didn't you break this up?'

'Benton had it coming to her, Sir.'

'What rubbish you talk. Get on up to school and listen to me, Saunders, don't let me catch you in a position like this again. Go on,' he raised a warning finger. 'Not a word, boy. Not one word else you'll be up in front of the Headmaster.'

'I'm sorry, Sir,' Mark said. 'But I'm not going without Violette.'

Mr Davies took a deep breath, then, relented.

'In the car, Rachel. And you, Violette, go with your brother. And,' he warned, 'report to me at school.'

As suddenly as the whole thing had started, it was finished. Mark and Violette were left alone in the street, Mr Davies's car pulling away from them and charging up the road to the school.

'Don't say anything,' Violette said miserably.

Mark shook his head.

'What is there to say?'

They walked together. Violette dabbed at her face with her handkerchief.

'Has all the blood gone?'

He nodded.

She raked her fingers through her hair, tidied her blouse

and jumper, brushed at her skirt.

'I dunno about you,' Mark said when they parted. 'But if you ask me, the whole world's gone stark staring mad.'

Then he left her.

Mark made enquiries at school. Finally, he found out that Janis had been seen collecting for the striking miners.

'If you'd waited and found out what she was talking about,' he said later, 'there wouldn't have been a fight and then there wouldn't have been all this trouble.'

'There would have been a fight. Whatever I'd done there'd have been a fight. She was out for a fight.' She reflected a moment. 'And so was I.'

The morning had been unpleasant. On reflection, Mr Davies had considered it wiser to report the whole matter to the Head. There had been an acid interview and a letter was to be sent to both girls' parents.

'What do you think Dad'll say?' Mark asked.

Violette grimaced.

'Oh, I know what he'll say. He'll read it, put it on the table then say "Right, well. Good. Good" and that'll be that.' She stared at the ground, tears pricking her eyes. 'He doesn't care about anything any more. Not since Mum went.'

'Don't you think they would have split up anyway?'

Violette glanced at him in surprise.

'Split up? Why should they?'

'Well, they were always rowing, weren't they?'

She opened her mouth to deny this but memory caught her small blows. Yes, they *had* rowed a lot. Shouting, banging doors and, worst of all, at night, the long long humming of talk, rising and falling, the bitterness seeming to seep through the walls into the other rooms.

'Yeah, well.'

She suddenly felt so tired she could have melted.

The day lasted for ever. This new trick of time wasn't a thing she cared for. How had it gone so fast before?

She didn't wait for Mark. He rampaged home with his pals. Rachel Benton eyed her from the far side of the English block but neither girl made any move towards the other.

Violette went through the school gates and started down the road for home. She thought she would run away but there was no point. No-one would even notice. Certainly no-one would care. She thought of her Granny. Oh well, her Granny would care. She could see the concerned blue eyes, the fretful face, but, she wasn't her Granny's daughter.

It would be something to think about over a cup of coffee perhaps and then her Gran would put her out of her mind, as her Dad had done and as her mother had done.

She scowled.

Her mother had done a bit more than put her out of her mind. She had put her out of her life.

A hand touched her shoulder. A familiar voice said, 'Violette,' and Violette knew it was her mother.

Chapter Four

Violette turned to face her mother, hoping against hope she had come to tell her she was returning home. She was startled by the change in Janis. She looked so different. Younger, almost, but – Violette looked at her – what was it . . . where was the difference?

She gave up.

'Mother.'

Janis frowned.

'Oh, come on, Violette. Don't be so stuffy. There's no need to be like that with me.'

'Like what?'

'So formal. As if I was just an acquaintance.'

Violette traced an intricate pattern in the loose gravel chips with the tip of her shoe.

'Look,' Janis started. 'I want to talk to you, OK? I want another go at explaining things. I don't feel I made all that good a job making it clear to you why I was going. Why I went. But –' she looked at her daughter. 'I think it can't be that difficult to understand. After all, you were there at that . . . that scene with your father.'

Violette said nothing.

Janis persevered, going into details Violette closed her ears to. Each time her mother paused for breath, she looked at the girl for approval, understanding, some sign even that she had spoken but Violette could do nothing. She felt so against what her mother had done, she couldn't even begin to understand Janis's reasons, couldn't begin to accept any explanation.

'For heaven's sake,' Janis said at last. 'I can see I was wrong to come. I'm sorry I did come now. Sorry I wasted my breath on you. I should have left well enough alone but I thought . . . I thought you'd understand, Violette. I thought I could turn to you and that you'd help me.'

Violette laughed.

'You thought all that would happen in this little bit of time?'

Her mother looked away.

'How odd,' the girl went on. 'If I'd been you, I think I would have wanted us to be upset. Have wanted us to miss you.'

'Well, you're wrong,' her mother said fiercely. 'I don't want that at all. I want you to adjust, that's what I want. To understand. I want you to be happy.'

'Happy? Happy? You want us to be happy? Let me tell you how happy I am, mother. You took on the job of marriage, didn't you? You married my Dad. I didn't. You had me and Mark. I didn't. *You* are supposed to be the mother. I'm not. But that's what you've made me. You've made me a mother, Mother.'

Janis pulled back from the girl.

'Now, look . . .' she started.

'No, you look,' Violette scrambled on. 'Do you know who cooks the dinner when we get home at night? I'll tell you. Me. Do you know who does the shopping at the weekend? I'll tell you. Me. I do. Do you know who has to make sure there are clean clothes – for everyone? Me.

38

Me. Me.'

Janis pulled a face.

'Oh, come on, Violette. Honestly. If you're doing all that, it's because you want to do it. No –' as Violette began to speak. 'No, you listen to me. Mark and your Dad have got arms and legs just as you have. Why shouldn't you all take it in turns to cook and shop and clean? There's no law says that men can't do these things. Not as I know to, anyway. No. Don't try and make me feel guilty. I had enough of that with your Dad. I'm finished with guilt.'

'You might as well finish with us, then, as well. Keep phoning and appearing like a genie. What use is that? Who wants it, mother?' She paused. 'Or perhaps you don't want to be called "mother" any more? Perhaps I should call you "Janis".'

'Actually, I was going to ask you about that. Now you mention it, yes, I would rather you called me Janis.'

Violette found she could hardly breathe, despite the soft clear air and lovely quality of light. There should have been plenty of air but she couldn't seem to get any of it.

Janis sighed as she saw the girl's face.

'Oh, love,' she began. 'Love, don't make it any more difficult for me than it is. I've come to you because I need some help. If I'd wanted all this –' she threw her arms wide as if to embrace the street, the town, as well as her daughter, 'then I could have got it from my own mother.'

Violette thought bitterly that at least Janis didn't have to call *her* mother by her christian name.

'Your mother was trying to stick up for you this morning.'

Janis made an odd throw-away movement.

'Violette, I need documents. They're in the house. I don't want to go and ask your Dad for them. Not yet.' She paused. 'But I do need them. I need my driving licence, my birth certificate, my marriage certificate, oh, all sorts of things. They're all together in the . . .'

'I know where they are. I live there, remember? I've always lived there. It's you that's left.'

'I know. I know.' Janis made a soft placatory gesture, as if she would stroke the girl's face but Violette pulled away from her.

'Now why are you looking at me like that?' Janis allowed her hand to drop. 'If you don't want to help, don't want to see me, don't want to do anything for me at all, then don't. For God's sake, just say so and I'll go. What I don't want is you judging me all the time. Anyone would think I was Lucretia Borgia the way you're all going on.'

Violette stopped herself retaliating. She began to walk down the road. Janis fell into step beside her.

'Well?' she demanded. 'I'm not going to beg . . . I've told you . . . and listen, if you don't want to help, I'll understand. God knows I'll understand. I mean . . . what I mean is that no matter what you do, Violette, I'll always love you.'

This struck Violette as almost blackmail.

'Love me?' she repeated, in rising fury. 'Love me?'

'Yes, love you. I do love you and even if you don't want to help, I'll still love you but I'm not going to beg and I'm not going to hang around. Just make up your mind what you want to do and tell me.'

'You're damn right I should tell you what I want to do.' Violette yelled suddenly, careless of the people passing them. 'I want to . . . I want to . . . make you go back to Dad, make you . . .' Her distress was so great the words jammed behind her tongue. 'I . . .' she tried again. 'I hate you. I really and truly hate you.' And then the tears came and scalded her cheeks.

'But why do you hate me?' her mother cried and the pain in her voice was as great as her daughter's. 'Why do you hate me? What have I done to you? I love you. I want to be with you.'

Violette made a harsh raw sound at this.

'I do. Just because I'm not going to be with you all the time, it doesn't mean I don't want to be with you at all. Oh, Violette, listen to me. You would have probably gone anyway in two years. University, marriage, who knows? You would have left me. You would have gone without a backward glance.' She checked the girl's sudden words. 'You know you would, Violette. Look –' She stopped, tired and unhappy. 'I'm going. I'll see you again when . . . when things have settled down a bit. It doesn't matter about the papers. I'll ring and ask your Dad if I can come and get them. He won't say "No". It was just me. Just my stupidity.'

There was silence as the girl and the woman both sought to control themselves.

'All right,' Violette announced. 'You win. I'll get you the papers.'

'They're in the cardboard cylin–'

'I've told you. I know where they are.'

Another silence.

'Do you want them all?'

'Yes.'

'What – our birth certificates as well?'

Janis nodded.

'Yes, those as well.'

They were tired. Both of them were tired. Violette rubbed her hands up and down her face.

Janis reached out and gently cupped the girl's cheek in the palm of her hand.

'Violette,' she half echoed, half whispered from her own confused and painful feelings. 'Wherever shall we end up?'

Then, she slipped her arm through her daughter's.

'Come on. Let's go for a cup of coffee.'

'No,' Violette muttered. 'Let's not go anywhere together.'

They walked to the town without speaking further. Violette could smell the perfume her mother was wearing. The heaviness of the scent was almost physical. Violette knew that when her mother had gone, the perfume would still cling to her coat and to her clothes. When she went to bed, she knew she would smell it in her own hair, on her hands, her cheeks , almost on her very breath.

At the end of the street leading to their house, they stopped.

'Are you sure you won't come for coffee?'

The girl shook her head.

'Then I won't come any further,' Janis said.

'So when shall I give you these papers you're desperate for?' Violette asked with untidy aggression. 'I mean, I thought you'd want me to rush in and bring them straight out to you.'

'No,' Janis shook her head. 'I don't want you to do that.'

She thought for a moment, her head tilted to one side, her clear eyes finding pleasure in the day.

'I won't hang about. But what you could do is get out to see me tonight.'

All at once, it seemed to Violette that this was what the papers were really about.

'Get out to see you where?' she asked with caution.

Janis grinned.

'Don't laugh but I've got a part in a . . . well, you remember the play I told you about?' She rushed on, not waiting for an answer. 'It's that one. It's a sort of political protest play. No,' she corrected. 'It is a political protest play and I've got a part in it. It's just women, you know. Just a group of women – but it's a good play. Strong. Meaningful.'

Violette winced. Meaningful? She wondered what 'meaningful' meant.

'Are they the same women who used to come round to the house?'

Janis nodded.

'I don't know why you have to mix with that lot.'

The little bond between them stretched and snapped.

'They've been more supportive than you,' Janis retorted. 'Oh God. I'm sorry, love. I'm sorry. I didn't mean that.'

Violette burst into tears.

Janis stood back, appalled.

'Don't cry like that.' She took Violette into her arms but after a few seconds, the girl became aware that her mother was uncomfortable. As Janis dabbed helplessly at Violette's tears, she tried to cling to her but Janis resisted. Not with force but by backing away, easing herself to one side, so that she almost began to seem like a woman looking on.

Violette felt the warmth between them drain away. Even the physical warmth vanished as their bodies lost contact. Now, she let her mother go.

Standing alone, Violette took deep steadying breaths. She forced the tears to stop. She was crying too much. She looked at her mother through the last of her tears. Her head felt hot and heavy and there was a bad insistent pain banging behind her eyes.

She lifted a hand and rubbed her forehead.

Janis waited, then volunteered, 'I'll be at the Social Club in South Elms.'

Violette thought of the desolation that was South Elms.

'And that's where your play is?'

Her mother nodded.

'Yes.'

Violette recognised now that the change in Janis which had shocked her was a deep change. She had thought when Janis first appeared there might still be the old relationship between them. Now, she could see it was dead. Whatever might exist between her mother and herself would have to be forged anew, and forged out of unknown material.

'Very well, mother . . . Janis. When shall I come?' she said now.

'If you come about eight, you could stop on and see the play,' her mother suggested. 'I'm not . . . I'm not very good yet. Anyway, if you come, you'll see for yourself.'

'I'd better go. Dad'll wonder where I am.'

Janis nodded.

'See you tonight, then.'

Violette turned away and set off down the street, miserable and confused. She half wished her mother had kept away and yet, the other part of her was glad she had come.

There was no father waiting when Violette got in. No father. No mother. No Mark. She wondered if Janis had known this would be the case. She felt as if she had lost the world. No-one cared, that was clear. Janis was all for Janis. Her Dad went around these days as if he existed in a vacuum and as for Mark, her brother kept out of the house as much as possible.

Standing in the hall, lit with sunshine and the scent of flowers, Violette felt deeply unhappy.

Wearily, she climbed the stairs to her room. It had been

a horrible, wretched day.

She went into her room and closed the door carefully behind her. The house would be deserted for many hours yet. She flung herself onto the bed and waited for the tears to come. When they did, she found almost a richness in weeping. After a little while and quite before she was ready, she found the tears drying up. She wanted to cry, needed to cry, but couldn't. She needed to be unhappy and miserable and she was, but still the tears refused to come.

Violette felt peevish. She determined that she would cry and set herself grimly to this end.

She thought of Janis, of the fight, of the hateful words Rachel had flung at her. She bit hard on her lips, dug her nails into the palms of her hands.

Nothing.

There were no more tears.

She sat up then, rose and brushed her hair. She looked in the mirror and noticed how her eyes sparkled. She looked very well.

'Trust me,' she muttered.

Her cheeks had a faint pink flush on them and it suited her. She dabbed a finger tip in lip salve and smoothed it on her lips. There! Really, her lips were quite a good shape. She pouted at her reflection, then frowned and sighed.

Who cared?

The last thing she did was to wash her hands. She couldn't rid them of her mother's perfume.

By the time she had collected the papers her mother wanted, then changed for the evening, her headache had returned and she banged the dishes about with bad temper.

Later, her father wandered into the kitchen and stood watching her.

'Going out?' he asked, aware there was something different about her but not sure what.

Violette looked down at the clothes she had chosen with such care. He hadn't even noticed them.

She nodded.

'Yes, I'm going out.'

He turned and drifted back to the room.

She stared at the dirty sink water.

'Dad,' she shouted. 'I'll leave the pots for you and Mark to do. OK?'

The television answered her with a burst of sound.

Violette brought her hand down with such force it almost hurt her as it smashed into the warm greasy water. It flew everywhere, drenching her clean blouse, soaking her hair, dripping down her face.

Mark, coming in for another biscuit, said, 'That was a daft thing to do,' and left.

With exaggerated care, Violette dried her hands, dabbed at her hair and blouse. Now she would have to change.

She left everything where it was and changed for the third time that evening. Looking into the mirror, she didn't like what she saw. She paused a moment, then drifted out onto the landing. She leant over the banister and stood listening.

The television went on and on. For the first time, she was glad it pacified her father.

She hurried into her parents' bedroom. Avoiding looking at the bed, she crossed to the wardrobe and opened the door. The coat hangers flew under her fingers. There it was. She pulled out a linen trouser suit and the silk shirt her mother always wore with it then went back to her own room.

Violette put the clothes on, smoothing her hand over the

material, licking the creamy silk, almost expecting it to taste.

She laughed aloud. All at once she felt alive and it was good.

It was very very good.

Chapter Five

The pit dominated South Elms. From a long way away, Violette could see its black skeleton towering over the houses and fields. She felt nervous and unsure. She began to wonder if it had been wise to come.

The bus trundled along the country roads, drawing closer and closer to the little mining village. When Violette got off, she saw there was a steady stream of people going into the Club. All at once she wished she had left her mother's clothes in the wardrobe. Feeling hot and overdressed, she hurried across the road, towards the Club entrance, longing to be in, to be in somewhere.

Impatiently, she pushed at the heavy swing doors and stepped through them. Inside, people were moving across a small foyer, disappearing through other open doors. Violette followed but as she drew near to the opening, a voice halted her.

'Now then, my duck, are you a member?'

To make sure her attention was caught, a hand touched her arm.

Violette stopped and turned to look at the man sitting beside a small table. She wondered how she had missed seeing him.

'What?' she asked.

'Are you a member?' He was very patient.

She saw the table was covered in books and papers.

'You can't come in unless you're a member,' he went on in his steady unhurried voice. 'Are you a member?'

Violette shook her head.

'No. No, I'm not.'

'Then you can't come in, my girl.'

She was half turning to leave before she thought to tell him about her mother.

'I've come to see my mother. She's acting in the play tonight.'

'Ahhhh!' The man was happy now. 'You can come in, then. Why didn't you tell me that at first?'

He looked pleased that they'd found a way of letting her in.

'Just you go straight through them doors and ask at the Bar. She'll tell you where to go then. But still, all the same –' he was thoughtful. 'You'd best just sign this.' He pushed an open book across the table. 'Just to be on the safe side. Just here,' he pointed to the place. 'See. On that line. Sign there.'

She signed and when she looked at the signature, saw it was strong and complete.

It gave her confidence so that she walked into the room beyond the open doors with grace and ease. The place was packed full. A pall of blue smoke hung in the air. Every table was occupied by men and women laughing and chattering. Children raced up and down, shouting, calling out to each other. There were groups, standing, crushed in between the tables, all talking, smoking, drinking. Bursts of sudden laughter scored the air like harsh bells.

Violette realised she had actually taken a step or two backwards.

Her new confidence deserted her. She stood, uncertain now where to go, what to do, who to ask for directions in this full and noisy room. Wetting her lips, she moved forward. A drift of men away from the Bar gave her a chance. Walking over, she leant against the dark wood, her eyes taking in the sparkling glasses and upturned bottles of amber and gold. She could see her reflection in the mirrored wall and grimaced at it.

A large woman with thick dark hair stepped in front of her, automatically wiping down the bar top.

'What will it be?' she asked. Then, sharp-eyed, 'A lemonade, won't it?'

'I don't want anything,' Violette forced out. 'I just want to know where the play people are. The man outside said you'd tell me.'

The bar maid looked puzzled.

'The actresses,' Violette tried again. 'Where are they?'

'Ah!' the woman answered now, smiling. 'Them. They're round the back. That's where they are. Through that door, see.'

She turned and pointed.

Violette turned to look at the door. She could only just see it through the smoke and mass of bodies.

'Go on,' the bar maid urged. 'Through yonder door and straight down the corridor to the end. You can't go wrong.'

Violette stepped away from the bar, and started out across the crowded room. It took her ages to get even a little way.

'Gerron. Gerron. Gerron,' a voice cried out so loudly, it dominated all the other sounds.

More voices joined in, picking up the senseless refrain like a song.

'Gerron, gerron, gerron. Getgetget, withee, Alan. Wheyheyheyyy, look at him. He ain't wasting no time.'

Startled, Violette turned her head. A tableful of grinning faces stared back at her.

'He's come, duck,' one of the young men shouted. 'Never thee fear. Thy Knight in shining armour's right by you. It's your lucky day. Theer he is.' And the group yelped with laughter as a tall young man stepped in front of Violette.

'Are you lost?' he asked, smiling at her.

She looked up at him. He was so beautiful, she felt she could look at him for ever and ever. The dark crisp curls lying on his forehead. The brilliant blue eyes, the lovely straight lips. She checked herself scornfully. What was this? He was just a feller.

'Who're you looking for?' He tried again.

'No-one,' she said. 'I know where I'm going, thanks. I don't need any help.'

The cries of the other young men carried on and as he reached out and took her arm, they rose to a crescendo.

'That's right. Yon's the laddo, eh? Look at him. Yehhhhh. Go to it, Alan. Gerron then.'

He jerked his head.

'Ignore them.'

'I am.'

'Stick close to me,' he grinned. 'I'll take you round the back.'

She wondered how he knew she wanted to go round to the back of the hall.

'Really, it's OK,' she insisted. 'I know where to go.'

'I'll go first.' It was as if she hadn't spoken. 'Come on, you just stick close to me.'

They had to go past the table of young men and Violette wished more than anything in the world that she had not put on her mother's clothing. It stifled her. All at once, she hated the hall, hated the young men, hated the people, the sounds, the smoke, the smells. She just wanted to be at home.

They made their way round the ungainly stage that had been constructed out of boards and beer crates. Then, they were at the door and he was opening it for her, ushering her through.

'Straight down there. Last one at the end,' he pointed. 'You can't go wrong.' And he was gone, closing the door behind him.

The moment she was on her own, she felt alarmed. The corridor was dark and dirty. There was one window, high up, shadowed with cobwebs. Unshaded bulbs hung from the ceiling. Over everything hung a strong unpleasant smell of disinfectant.

Cautiously, she walked down the hall. She hesitated, at the last door looking over her shoulder. The far door she had just come through opened suddenly and with quick anxiety, she knocked on the one in front of her and pushed it open.

'Violette!' her mother's voice rang out. 'So you've made it. I am glad. Come on in. For heaven's sake . . .'

The amazement was mild.

'What are you wearing?' Her voice was light and amused. 'Aren't those clothes mine? Well, I don't need them. You're welcome to anything I've left.'

'I don't want anything you've left,' Violette said crossly. 'And I don't know why I'm wearing these. I think I must have had a brainstorm. I hate them. They're awful. I wish I'd never put them on.'

Violette unbuttoned the top of the blouse. It was choking her.

'Then why did you?' Her mother was edgy. 'You should have left them where you found them.'

'Yes. I should.'

Violette looked curiously around the room. It was a mess. Piles of clothes on chairs and more on the floor. An old piano. Vases of dusty paper flowers. Some battered Christmas garlands swinging across the ceiling.

'Is this freedom then?' she asked. 'This mess?' but before her mother could answer, there was another knock on the door and the tall young man from the hall stepped in.

'I've brought more copies of the script.' He spoke to Janis but looked at Violette.

'Just put them down, Alan,' Janis said wearily. 'Anywhere.'

Alan dropped the papers onto the piano.

'Now, who is this?' he asked, smiling. 'We all want to know. She's created a stir, she has.'

Violette felt sour, angry, and made to turn away from him but he smiled with such warmth and vigour, she found herself responding.

'You're really storming the South Elms Social Club you are, aren't you?' He walked over, holding out his hand. 'I'm Alan.'

He took her hand between his hands, rubbing his thumb over her skin.

'You leave her alone, Alan.' Her mother's voice made Violette jump. 'Stop teasing her.'

'The minute I know her name.'

'Violette. Her name is Violette and she's my daughter.'

'Well, Violette her daughter, I'm pleased to meet you.' He smiled at her again. 'Very pleased.'

'Behave yourself.' Janis was short with him. 'And in case you've forgotten, there's that stage to check yet.'

Violette had to pull her hand out of Alan's hands. She felt as if her fingers had twined round his, like a plant grown wild. She blushed.

Her mother was impatient.

'Now you're here, Violette, you might as well help me.

There's a lot to do.' She looked pointedly at Alan. 'A lot to do.'

'All right, all right.' The young man held his hands up in mock defence. 'I'm just going. OK?'

Janis turned away from him. He winked at the girl.

'See you later.'

Violette nodded, not knowing what else to do. Besides, she would like to see him again.

'Ready?' Her mother was waiting.

Violette jerked her attention away from Alan.

'Will you hear me read? I need to go through my part again.'

Suddenly, Janis was blazing with excitement.

'My part,' she laughed. 'I need to read my part.'

She talked on whilst Violette moved around the room, taking off her coat, hanging it up, getting a chair, then pulling it up to her mother and, finally, seating herself and holding out her hand for the script.

'I can't tell you what a difference this play has made,' her mother said now.

Violette looked at her mother. Yes, she could see the play had made a difference. Her mother looked deeper, more solid in her being. She wondered why.

'Hear me read, Violette.'

Violette watched the beautiful absorbed woman. She could see now how lovely her mother was. She wondered if *she* was beautiful and if she was, was it in the same way? All the same, she sat a little straighter. Alan had liked her. Again the hot colour swept up her neck and over her face.

'Come on then, Mum. Get on with it.'

Before they could start, the door crashed open and the rest of the women, old and young, poured in. Violette recognised many of them and it was clear from their greetings that they hadn't forgotten her.

They shouted with friendly good humour, drawing the girl into their ranks as if she had always been there. As if she meant to be there.

'Joining the Cause, are you?' they asked and without waiting for an answer, laughed slyly at her awkwardness.

Violette felt the same stifling drowning feeling she had always felt when they had met in the front room at home. She felt suddenly unhappy and didn't know why. It was just that . . . if she closed her eyes, she thought she was back at home, back in the time when they were still a family.

She became aware that Janis had been reading for some time.

'Erm . . .' she tried. 'Mum . . . Janis . . .'

Janis stopped, turning to her daughter, her face caught up in the story she was acting.

'Mum, I'm sorry. I wasn't listening.'

'Right.' A short pause. 'Right. I'll start again.'

This time Violette concentrated. She watched and listened. She saw the transformation. For Janis, the room disappeared. She became the woman in the play, torn with despair and rigid with anger. Her face changed, hardened.

She rose to her feet, flexing her body, ready to move into the climax of the scene. The other women looked at her, some with good nature, others with impatience.

'Why don't you put a sock in it?' one of them cried.

And another:

'Shut up, Janis. There's not only you here.'

Janis came out of the role almost as if in shock. Violette, sensing her fight the suddenness of return, touched her.

'It's all right, mother. It's OK.'

'Don't call me "mother".' The voice was flat and cold. 'How many times do you need telling?'

Violette drew back, stunned.

She felt tearful and fragile.

'Come on, love.' One of the women seized her.

Violette felt like clinging to this woman.

'Come on. Don't look so hard done by. Out into the audience with you.' She laughed. 'You shouldn't take so much notice of her. Especially not just now. You know what it's like. Stage fright.' Now she smiled. 'Go on.' She patted the girl's bottom. 'You go out to the front. There's a row of seats saved. Grab one of them. Just sit back and enjoy yourself. Forget all this. Just enjoy the play.'

Violette made her way to the hall. She sat on the front row, miserable and upset. The room darkened and the actresses appeared.

For the next hour, Violette was caught up in the world in front of her. The boards creaked, smoke drowned the room but the women played as if they were alone, as if they were real, acting out their age-old story of loss and longing, of children and poverty, of men loved and men hated, of struggle, defeat, despair, of sisterhood, motherhood, of faith and broken trust.

At the end of the first act, the silent men, the standing women clapped as if they would bring the roof down.

The noise started again. Children spilt their orange juice, rattled their crisp packets. The barmaid served beer and cigarettes in the muted light. The talk rose and fell.

Violette stayed where she was. She didn't feel up to tackling her mother again. Now this first half was over, she was tired and impatient. She slumped on the chair, kicking against the nearest beer crate.

She wished she could get to her feet and leave but she felt inert. She couldn't be bothered to go and yet she hated to stay.

She banged forward and back in the chair. The man sitting next to her sighed at the irritation. He was a

56

middle-aged, self-contained man, dressed in clothes that were as out of place as Violette's own. Grey suit. Grey overcoat. White shirt. Neat tie. Wispy hair stranded over his head to hide the scalp that looked pink and silky.

Violette shuddered.

Now he smiled at her as if regretting his irritability.

'A pleasant evening,' he ventured.

She nodded, wondering if she could change seats but it was too late. The room darkened and the players were back. She couldn't concentrate for the man at her side. He was leaning forward, eyes swivelling from one woman to another but then he settled, his eyes fixed on her mother.

She felt it had been a bad decision to come. But then she heard her mother's clear voice and was, finally, despite herself, despite the man at her side, drawn in to the play by the power of Janis's performance.

Other voices broke in, took over, and Violette surfaced out of her intense absorption.

Idly, she glanced across the stage and with a jolt, found she was staring at Alan. As she focused on him, she saw he was watching Janis with a dreamy intensity. She looked from him to her mother. There was an awareness about Janis. Was it because Alan was there?

As if Alan had felt her gaze, he looked up and across at her. He grinned and winked. She couldn't smile back but dropped her eyes to the dirty boards of the stage.

She wondered if there was anything going on between him and her mother. Her attention turned back to the play.

As her mother finally stepped down and walked into the darkness, Violette felt a great separation from her.

Then it was over and the lights went up. The women ran back and joined together, laughing, bowing their heads, clasping their hands in triumph.

Violette was more touched by the play than she would

acknowledge. The idea of sisterhood, of feminine solidarity based on a reaching-out love was new to her.

She moved restlessly. It was a play. Yes, a good play. A warm, caring play but a play. She felt tired but stood and applauded with the rest of the audience.

There were no bouquets but when Janis's name was called out, she stepped forward and the clapping grew louder. Sometime during all this, the grey man slipped away.

Violette was relieved when she saw he had gone. He'd made her uneasy.

Then it was over and the audience dispersed, the actresses went back to their dressing room.

Violette trailed backstage to give her mother the flat packet of papers, wanting it out of her hands, wanting to be away.

She was aware of Alan in the room the moment she stepped through the door. He was collecting the scripts, talking first to one woman, then to another. With quiet authority he discussed venues, timetables, transport.

When he left, he winked at her but she turned from him.

'I'll be back,' he said, almost as if he were making her a promise.

She shrugged this away. What was he to her? What was she to him?

As Janis washed and changed, Violette searched her bag. The packet of papers had settled at the bottom and she had to drag it out. She stood with it in her hand.

Her mother sat down and slipped her shoes on. She looked exhausted.

'You're tired,' Violette offered.

'Yes.'

Janis leant back in the chair.

'Let me give you the papers and then I'm off. I can't

stand it here.'

Janis held out her hand and with a sense of relief, Violette placed the package into it.

'There,' she said. 'That's what you wanted.'

Janis looked at the packet.

'Yes. This is what I want.'

'Are you getting a divorce?'

Her mother didn't answer, saying instead, 'Sit down a minute. There's a bus soon. It stops right outside. You've got time to sit.'

Violette didn't want to sit down. She didn't want to stay in the room at all.

'How are you getting home?' she asked.

'Alan's taking me.'

The girl was silent. So Alan was taking her. Well, let him. She wanted nothing to do with any of them. She wished she could have met Alan any place other than here. Here he was involved with her mother and her friends. Violette thought her life would never be long enough to take in Janis's friends.

And then Alan was back.

Janis glanced up at him. She yawned and stretched.

'Do you want to come with us? You can if you want although we're not going yet.'

Violette shook her head.

'No. I'm going now.'

'Please yourself.'

Janis stretched again. Stretching, she demanded attention. Alan certainly gave it her, Violette noticed with quick anger.

But her mother's skin was touched with little lines. Perhaps he didn't care Janis was so much older. She knew Janis wouldn't care. You were older. So what?

'Are you sure you'll be OK?' Alan asked. 'Sure you don't

want to come with us?'

'No, I don't want to come with you. I'll be all right.'

'Well, watch your step,' Alan warned. 'It can be a bit . . .'

'Do stop worrying,' Janis said impatiently. 'The bus stop is right outside. I'm sure Violette can manage to get there on her own. You men,' she swept on, 'I swear you'd have us back in the bustle and fettered to the fireside at the drop of a hat.'

'I only asked.' Alan spread his hands out. 'If she thinks she'll be all right, then that's OK by me.'

Violette felt like saying she had a tongue in her own head.

'I'll be off, then.'

'Thanks for bringing those papers . . . and thanks for staying to watch the play.' Janis paused. 'I wanted to ask you . . . well, I wondered . . . what did you think of me? Of my acting?'

'You were all right.'

Violette wanted to go.

'Yes, well, thanks for the unstinting support,' her mother said drily.

There was no point in answering. Violette was glad to escape from the claustrophobic staleness of the room.

She plunged down the dark corridor. In her haste she missed the door leading back into the bar room. She hesitated but as she hesitated, the air grew fresher. It was very dark, so dark she could hardly see. She glanced over her shoulder, wondering if perhaps she ought to turn back but it seemed easier to go on.

Double doors were in front of her and, laying her hands on the iron rod, she hefted it up, pushed, and the door opened.

The air poured in. It spilt over her face and body cooling her. Spirits higher, she slipped into the night. From where she stood, she could see the glow of a street lamp. She could distinguish the greyness of the path leading to the road.

She started to move towards the lamp, to the street, to the bus stop where people were waiting. She was elated at being free of the Social Club.

But, before she could clear the bulk of the building, with terrifying, heart-stopping suddenness, a man's arms, legs, body were all over her, his tongue thrusting and pushing at her closed mouth.

She was in the middle of a nightmare.

Chapter Six

There were a few seconds when Violette couldn't react. She thought she must be dreaming. This was what happened to other people – not to her. She couldn't understand it. Her thoughts were flying, racing, tearing down one path in her mind and charging up another and yet, yet, her body was still. Just for those few seconds.

Then the stillness passed and she began to struggle, pulling away from the man with all her strength. She was young and strong and she used that youth and strength. She could smell him. It drove her mad. Smell tobacco on his breath. Stuff on his face. It gave her impetus.

'Jesus!' the exclamation tore from the man's mouth.

In a frenzy of panic, Violette lashed out. The man was silent now but she could hear his breathing. It caught in his throat. He coughed. She hated the cough, the throat, the mouth. He gave a shout of laughter. Again, his lips suckled her own. She wanted to be sick. She wrenched her face to one side, her own breath tearing through her mouth, rasping, whistling thinly into the silence.

She could see him in her mind's eye. She didn't want him. Didn't want him to touch her.

It was the man in the grey suit, with the hair striped over his scalp. She was sure it was.

'For God's sake, you bitch. Stop it. It's only a bit of fun.'

She knew it wasn't the grey man then. This voice was rough with a strong local accent.

'Here. Here. Pack it in.'

She fought harder.

'Bloody 'ell' the voice complained, ragged and yet still amused as if the whole thing were one big joke. 'I'd never have thought you had it in yer, you little sod.'

The struggle went on. Such was the force of her resistance now, he wasn't trying to do anything but restrain her.

He caught her face in his hand and forced it still. She felt like a dog trapped by the hand of its owner. He bent his head to kiss her and she drew her lips back over her teeth. Then, they both heard it. A slight sound. She twisted her head to the light. There were helmets. Police. Oh, thank God, there were the police. On the far pavement. If she could only make them hear – get to them, they would help her. She knew they would help her.

She strained to free herself – why was she so aware of every line of his body, tracing and doubling her own? Why did she feel so sick? As she tried to scream, the man smacked a hand over her mouth and dragged her back into the darkness of the wall.

Now there was a difference. He pulled her back as if she were a straw. No more pretending. No more play fighting. He lifted her bodily from the ground.

'Shut up,' he whispered. 'Shut your bloody mouth else I'll kill yer.' And, trembling, she stopped the scream in her throat.

All at once the whole thing had grown worse. She felt in more real danger than before. Bad. Terrible. His smell had changed to a sour muskiness. She felt he was scared now. Not just her. Him too. He was scared so it had to be that much more dangerous.

'A bit of bleeding fun, that's all I wanted.'

He was angry. Angry.

'Can't tek a bleeding joke, that's your trouble. You just keep your sodding mouth shut. Fetch them coppers over here and you're for it.'

He was whispering straight into her ear.

'For it,' again. 'Yes . . .' – long word. 'For It.'

She could feel his lips against her skin. Then he poked his tongue down and around her ear, biting at the lobe hard enough to make her jerk against him.

'I like that,' he whispered. 'Let's do that some more.'

His breathing changed. It grew heavy, hard. She felt his mouth on her neck, felt him nuzzling her, then biting, then sucking. He was sucking the skin on her neck. She could have fainted with horror.

She jerked her head backwards and forwards trying to escape, trying to get her mouth free of the confining hand.

'Oh God. Oh God.'

That was all she could hear in her head.

'Oh God. Oh God.'

He was moving round her. Moving to face her. There seemed no end to this terror. Now, he pressed his body into hers and still his mouth . . . his mouth . . . went on and on, sucking and nuzzling and searching.

'Oh God. Oh God.'

They were leant against the wall, as if they were lovers, him pushing his hand into her face. His body measuring her length. His knee jammed now between her legs, forcing her legs apart.

She murmured in pain and his grip on her tightened.

'You and me,' he whispered. 'We're gonna have a nice time.'

She could have died with terror and pain. Died with the shame of what he was trying to do to her. She tried to put her legs together but he wouldn't let her. She thought of the trouser suit. Oh God, she was glad she had worn it. Irrelevancies. Glad she had worn Janis's trouser suit. No, no, no, not an irrelevancy. It was the trousers.

Really, she could have laughed. She felt hysteria forcing up into her mouth. Laughed. She could have laughed.

Then, when his hand was pushing at the soft waistband, pulling and squeezing and pushing, he was hit by a whirlwind.

Something tore him from her. She heard the snap, felt the snap of the waistband crack back against her body and he was gone.

'I'll knock your rotten head off.'

Whose voice was that? She knew that voice.

There was a brief noisy scuffle and then she heard footsteps running away and Alan was bending over her, trying to take her into his arms. She could have been sick. More arms. More maleness.

'Leave me alone. Leave me alone.'

She backed away from him.

'Just leave me alone. Please.'

Alan stepped back.

'Sod it all. I *knew* I should've seen to you.' He paused. 'Do you want me to get the police?'

Violette recoiled in horror.

Want the police? More men? Dear God, not now.

'No. No.' she said. 'No-one. Please. No-one.'

The young man hesitated.

'Janis is still in the Club. Shall I fetch her?'

This seemed to Violette a thousand times worse than the police.

'No, no. I want no-one, nothing. I'm —' she stumbled. 'I'm going home.'

What time was it? How long had it taken? It didn't seem

to be short of a lifetime but looking round her, the world was the same.

Violette didn't know which direction she was facing. She stood on the path not knowing what to do and the moon scudded in and out of the clouds. At last Alan took hold of her arm. She felt burnt, and pulled violently away.

Alan held on to her.

'Down here,' he said. 'Straight on. I'll lead you out to the bus stop.'

Violette took a step as if she had no idea what a step was. Alan steadied her.

'Don't pull away. You're all right with me. You know you are. Go on. Keep going. Straight down the path.'

She stumbled down the path. Alan tried to guide her but she kept pulling away from him.

And then she could see the bus stop. See people standing there as if nothing had happened. She could even see the bus.

She turned to the anxious young man.

'Do I look all right?'

He thought she looked very beautiful and very vulnerable – and sick. His heart ached for her.

'Let me come with you.'

'Oh God, no.'

He turned away.

'Do I look all right?' she demanded again. 'No-one would know, would they, looking at me no-one would know?'

Alan shook his head.

'No. No-one would know.'

She turned from him. He stood there until she reached the end of the path and stepped into the light. Once she was in the light of the street lamp, she turned to face him.

'Thank you. Thank you.'

He nodded.

Violette left him then, running for the bus. She was the last on. He could see her moving down the aisle, hurrying to the back. He hoped she would be all right. He wondered if he should tell Janis but shrugged. Janis didn't live with the girl. There was nothing she could do.

He watched the bus disappear. That was the end of that night. For Violette it seemed the night was only just beginning.

She sat on the back seat of the bus trying to put it all together. What had happened, when. She winced away from the memory of the man behind the Club. Her body felt raw and used. She had to do something, anything, to take away the feel of his hands and his tongue and his lips and everything – his body.

She started to shiver.

The bus rumbled its way along the country roads. It stopped every few minutes to pick up and drop off. Violette was astonished at the world going about its business. Didn't they know what had happened?

She stared into the window. Her reflection stared back. She didn't look any different. She hadn't got a mark on her forehead or even bruises. Her hair was a bit untidy but that was all.

She couldn't accept there was no change, not after all she had been through – yet there wasn't, she could see there wasn't.

She felt itchy. She looked down at the suit jacket. How she hated it.

With sudden decision, Violette took it off and threw it over the seat beside her. The blouse shone. She felt cooler, seeing the shining whiteness in the window. Again, she stared at her reflection. Scrabbling in her bag until she found a comb, she combed her hair over and over and over. Wiped her face and neck and ear with a tissue and dropped the tissue beneath her feet. More and more tissues until her skin hurt. She scrubbed at her lips until they bled and she was glad to see them bleed. Then she bit them, licked them, spat on her hands and rubbed her sore lips until spit and blood dried under her fingers.

Again, she peered into the window. Were they marks on her cheeks? Had he marked her? She couldn't see properly. She looked as if she had black holes in her face. How could she have? What had he done to her?

She filled the black holes with her fingers.

Turning over the events of the night, she realised one fact. She had no idea what her attacker looked like. She shrank away from the phrase 'her attacker' as if he were hers and no-one else's. Someone joined on to her, part of a joint effort. Hers. *The* attacker. That was it. Not *her* attacker. *The* attacker.

She moaned and a woman further down the bus turned round.

She didn't know him, didn't know what he looked like. She could bump into him in the town and apologise and she wouldn't know it was him – but *he* would. He would know. Know the feel of her, the smell of her. Know that he had . . . she baulked . . .

He would know and she wouldn't. Now it began to seem worse than ever. Would he follow her? Had he got a car? Was he behind the bus now, waiting for her to get off?

She twisted round and stared out of the back window. There were no cars behind.

She swallowed hard.

This wouldn't do. She would have to control her thoughts.

And then before she knew it, they were in the town. Street lights, people, cars, all moving.

Violette hurried, hurried down the aisle. She leapt off at the station, jumping out whilst the bus was still moving. The driver bawled at her 'Stupid cow,' but she didn't care.

The cool air was so good. She watched the bus jolt away. She was hot. Tired. Her heart was thumping. She needed movement.

She was glad she had kept her trainers on. Now she tried an experimental jog. No-one took notice of joggers any more.

Then she was running. She raced past the emptying public houses. Hands reached out to catch her but she avoided them.

Unexpectedly she felt a surge of sheer pleasure. The night was cool and clear. It was great to be pounding on the pavements. She wished his face was under her feet. She imagined that unknown face in the muck. It made her feel good.

A car pulled alongside her.

'Now then, Miss, what do you think you're doing at this time of night?'

'Jogging,' she shouted. 'Jogging' and she leapt in the air as if to catch a star.

The two policemen grinned.

'Come on. Come on,' they chided. 'Time you was home. It's not safe to be out at this time of night. Jogging!' but they kept smiling.

The pleasure lasted right until Violette was putting her key in the lock. The door opened suddenly, pulling the key from her hand before she had chance to turn it.

Her father stared at her.

'Where have you been? Do you know what time it is?'

'Oh, Dad,' the girl groaned. 'Not now, Dad, please.'

She started to tremble. Just a little bit. Her lips first. Then her hands. She held her hands up and looked at them. She was astonished. She held them out for her father to see. He reached out to her.

'What's wrong?' he asked. 'What's happened?'

Now she was shaking all over and could not stop. She could *not* stop.

Her Dad put his arm round her shoulders and guided her into the house.

He roared for Mark and when Mark staggered to the head of the stairs, ordered, 'Ring your Granny. Ask her to come over.'

Violette was aware of the fire being stoked. Aware of the flames reaching into the chimney, dragging down with them treacherous sparks. The sparks turned into Alan and Janis.

Then her Granny was at her side.

'Come on, let's get you to bed, Violette.'

The soft voice persuaded and cajoled until Violette was tucked up in bed.

On and on the questions went.

'Did anything happen? You can tell me. Tell me. Did anything happen?'

'Nothing happened. No. Nothing happened. Nothing happened.'

The thoughts of men, walking, talking. On, on, on.

'I'm telling you. Nothing happened.'

'Are you sure?'

'Yes. I'm sure.'

By morning, Violette was calmer. When she woke, she had a headache and a cough.

Her father was sitting in the chair next to the bed. He was asleep but as she turned over, his eyes opened.

'OK, ducks?'

Yes, she was OK.

'I must have caught a chill.' She was coughing.

'I'm going to ask just this one more time,' he said, and turned his face away from her. Now why did he do that, she wondered. 'Did anything *happen* to you last night?'

He couldn't go on because he had no words to go on with.

'I . . . I keep telling you. I just felt very hot. I think I was sickening for this . . . this chill. That's all.'

He wanted to believe her. Yes, he decided he would believe her. He was relieved. Now he patted her. Patted her arm.

'Are you sure?'

She lost her temper then, shouting at him until he apologised.

'There can't be much wrong with you,' he grinned. 'Not when you can put on a display like that.'

She couldn't really smile properly but he grinned at her. Yes, she could be fierce now, the smile said. She had his permission to be fierce. Now he knew for sure that nothing had happened. She was to stay in bed. No, he insisted. He would fetch her some breakfast.

Then, her Gran was back.

'I told you she was all right, Peter. Stop worrying. There's nothing to worry about.'

When he'd gone, she said, 'Nothing happened down there, did it? Down . . . there –' she nodded at Violette's body.

The words made her long for a bath.

'I'm fine, I keep telling you. What do you want me to do to convince you? I was just unwell last night. That's all it was.'

They looked at each other.

'Just so long as we know,' her Gran said obliquely and it was left.

When she'd gone, Violette started to think of her

mother. She wanted her mother. She didn't want Janis. She wanted, needed her own dear mother and knew she couldn't have her. Not the same mother. Not ever again.

'You stopping there all day?' Mark's voice cut through her thoughts. 'What were you doing last night, anyway?'

Her brother lounged against the door.

'I thought Dad was gonna kill every living thing between here and the end of the Universe,' he grumbled. 'Heck, V. It's bad enough here without Mum. What do you want to go messing things up for? Now I've got to be in at "a proper time",' he mimicked.

He was resentful.

'I wish Mum would come back. You seem to do nothing but get into trouble since she left.'

He slouched out of the room.

Violette sat up. Did she? Get into trouble all the time? Just because Janis wasn't there?

She slid out of bed. By the time her Granny came back with a tray of food, she was dressed.

'I'm OK, Gran. I've got to go to work.'

A day in the house would kill her.

'I can't afford to lose that job.'

'You don't have to go to work,' her Dad said when she appeared. 'Take the day off for once.'

'I can't take it off. It's only a Saturday job. There's too many after them. Stay off once and that's your lot. Your job's gone. They'll give it to someone else.'

She grumbled on, frightened to let silence develop, forcing herself to eat.

As soon as she paused, her father cut in.

'Violette –' He was hesitant. 'Listen. I'm not sure how much of what you said you meant last night.'

God, what had she said?

'About your mother, I mean. I don't want you to hate her.'

She almost laughed with relief.

'I don't hate her. Whatever did I say to make you think that?'

Her Dad looked unhappy.

'It was all garbled, mixed up,' he said, miserably. 'I couldn't really make it all out except that you threw her jacket away because you . . . oh, something or other. It was all mixed up. Anyway, I just got the impression that you hated her. Your Mum. You hated her.'

'I don't hate her.' Violette was appalled. She didn't hate her. Did she? 'No, I don't hate her. I wasn't well last night, that's all it was. I forgot the jacket. Well, she wasn't bothered about having it anyway.'

'That's the truth then, is it?' He was very sharp-eyed now.

She grew careful, suspicious.

'Oh sure, that's the truth.'

She wondered what would happen if she did tell him the truth. What were his options? If she told him about the man, what would he or could he do? She wondered really if anything at all would happen. Did parents and children ever speak the truth to each other? Was it always necessary to lie? When she looked back, an unbroken string of lies separated her from her mother and father. She had never realised that before. Never even thought of it in that way but it was true.

Lies, lies and lies.

For the first time, she began to see a tiny ray of light shining through Janis's new philosophy.

She would be herself, she decided. As from this day, she wouldn't think of herself as a daughter at all, then she would never need to lie again.

'Will you mind doing the shopping, then?' her father asked. He saw her face. 'Only if you feel all right, that is,' he added hastily. 'I mean, don't do it if you don't want to. It's just that if you didn't mind, I could get a bit done in the house.'

Violette bent her head.

'No, Dad,' she lied. 'I don't mind doing the shopping.'

They smiled at each other. These two liars. They both smiled.

Chapter Seven

As soon as Violette stepped in through the open back door of the shop, she sensed change.

Mrs Bartlett turned from the coffee cups and said briskly 'Only just on time, Violette. I had rather hoped you'd be early this morning.'

Violette said nothing. She took off her coat and hung it up.

Mrs Bartlett handed her a clean overall.

'We've got a new girl today.'

Violette frowned. So that was the change.

'There's too much work for just you and me,' Mrs Bartlett went on. 'What with all the wool coming in during the week and this, that and the other, well, I told her. I said "Miss Porter, unless I have extra help on a Saturday, well, I don't know what will happen," I told her. "Don't hold me responsible for it all," is what I said. "Because it's more than one person can do to see to everything in this shop." Well, she saw the sense of that, didn't she. "I'm sure I don't expect that of you, Mrs Bartlett" she said, a bit sniffy. "I shall come in myself." "Ho, yes," I thought. "I've heard that story before. Come in yourself, indeed. Half past four in an afternoon, that's what I thought," and she said "You needn't look like that, Mrs Bartlett . . ."'

Mrs Bartlett's voice droned on and on. Violette prepared

the coffee. It was cooling by the time the manageress had finally stopped.

'Anyway, the upshot was "Get another girl" she said, so I did.'

As if on cue, a voice chimed in 'Morning, Vi,' and with a sinking heart, Violette turned to see Rachel Benton standing there.

'A bit of a surprise this, eh?' Rachel grinned.

Violette wondered if she could face a whole day of Benton's company.

'Oh! So you know each other then? You should have said. Letting me go on like that and knowing all the time she was here.'

Mrs Barlett stared at Violette with sudden dislike.

'I didn't know she was here.'

'Hmmmm. Well, come on, get a move on, the pair of you. Really, you girls think you can earn your money by just standing chattering.'

Violette and Rachel went through into the shop. Violette had always enjoyed the first minutes in the unlit rooms.

The sharp smell of wool. The dustiness of the materials and cottons. The glittering strands of sequins. The tumbled lengths and rolls of scarlet, blue, lemon and white.

'If you want to know anything, ask Violette,' Mrs Bartlett said, her earlier dislike forgotten.

The two girls started to tidy up the stock. Mrs Bartlett sorted the cash float into the till. The lights were switched on and the day started.

They were hard at it most of the morning. Mrs Bartlett sent them for their coffee break as if the owner had personally tried to steal the fifteen minutes from them.

'The customers will just have to wait,' she said with gloomy satisfaction. 'I'm sure I can't be held responsible if they have to wait. Only three preople on and two of them mere children,' she emphasised. 'Untrained. That's what I tell them. I have to do everything myself, I say.'

She tut-tutted in sympathy with her own complaints.

'Would it be better if we went one at a time for coffee?' Violette proferred but Mrs Bartlett swept the suggestion contemptuously to one side.

'Oh dear me, no. I'm afraid if you want to be a manageress such as I am, my dear, you'll have to learn about forward planning.' She paused. 'I need to have slightly longer this morning for my break. I want to leave the shop with a clear mind. Not be everlasting worrying if one of you's having coffee and there's only one in the shop. No,' she finished. 'It's my eyes.' A faint line of worry creased her forehead. 'They're not at all what they used to be. I don't know . . .' she subsided unhappily.

'Your mouth is though,' Rachel murmured.

Violette glanced at her and then, before Mrs Bartlett could say anything, said, 'We'll go now. That way you'll be able to get out and back before lunch.'

The manageress's face brightened.

'Take your time,' she urged. 'Have your full fifteen minutes.'

The two girls went to the kitchen.

'She's stupid, that woman,' Rachel said, as she put the kettle on. 'Only three in the shop and she sends two out.'

Violette decided she wouldn't speak at all if she could help it.

'I saw you last night,' Rachel went on. 'We all did. Running through the town. Showing off.' There was a short silence as she lit the gas ring and placed the kettle on it. 'I don't know what you'll get up to next, Saunders, but you want to watch yourself. You can get into a lot of trouble going on the way you're going on.'

'Why don't you do us all a favour and drop dead?'

'You was seen as well outside the South Elms Social Club. Slumming, were you?'

'You ought to go and work for the paper. They wouldn't need any other reporters with you there. The eyes and ears of the world, that's you. It's a pity you've got nothing better to do than mind –'

'And there's your mother.'

'Lay off my mother!' Violette warned.

'Oh, I'll lay off her. Pity others can't. Lay off her.' There was such salaciousness in Benton's voice that Violette stared at her, wondering what she was getting at. 'What I mean is, it's a pity that boyfriend of hers can't . . . erm . . . lay' – she put a heavy emphasis on the word – 'lay off her'.

Violette's hands clenched.

'That Union lad,' the girl enlarged.

Benton tucked her chin in and managed to look almost as old as Mrs Bartlett.

'Like mother, like daughter, that's what everybody's saying. Her knocking off these young lads and you running about, trying to get the lads to run after you.'

Violette clenched her hands together and squeezed them hard. She knew if either hand were free, with or without her consent, it would fly across and smash into Benton's face.

She didn't want to lose her job for fighting.

'Still, if that's the sort of thing you like. You and your Mum.' Benton paused. 'There's a name for women like that though, isn't there? I mean, women like your mother. Cradle snatchers they call them, don't they? Yeah, cradle snatchers.'

Violette watched the narrow spiteful face. 'Yeah,' Benton went on. 'She wants to watch she doesn't get nappy rash.'

Violette turned from Rachel, not even wanting to look at

the girl. She placed her cup on the table, swallowed hard and then said, 'You're absolutely sick, Benton. You must be full of spite and hate.'

'It's not me that's sick. It's you. You and that mother of yours.'

Violette shook her head.

'No, we're not.'

Mrs Bartlett erupted into the kitchen.

'I said fifteen minutes, girls. Not seventeen.' She looked at them with sorrowful eyes. 'You see. I can't trust you, can I?'

Violette was glad to go through into the shop with the manageress. She felt as if Benton dirtied the air itself.

Mrs Bartlett bustled up and down until, satisfied at last, she called, 'I won't be long, dear.' She glanced over her shoulder. 'Keep an eye on that new girl. She doesn't seem all she should be, somehow.'

As Mrs Bartlett walked through the door, Rachel came into the shop.

'Just get on with your work, Benton,' Violette ordered. 'No more talking.'

Rachel opened her mouth to argue but Violette surprised herself by saying with ferocious dignity, 'I said no more talk.'

They worked in silence. The shop began to get quieter as twelve o'clock approached. Shortly before twelve, when Mrs Bartlett should have been back but wasn't, the door opened and when Violette looked up, she saw Janis and Alan gazing down the room at her. Both smiling, they walked towards her.

'I thought you'd be here,' Janis said. 'We've come to take you for lunch – and . . .' she paused for effect. 'To tell you my big news.'

Violette was swept up by her mother's enthusiasm.

'What big news?' She knew she was grinning. She was so glad to see Janis. And, a curly little thought, to see Alan.

'I've got a flat and a job,' Janis smiled. 'How about that?'

'Ohh, Mum,' Violette laughed. 'A flat and a job. Well, what can I say?'

She couldn't think of anything to say. A flat and a job. Janis beaming and twinkling away. Alan lighting up the shop simply by being there.

A flat and a job. What about them, now, then? Her and Mark, and her Dad. There wouldn't be room for them in the flat and the job.

The glow of shared happiness faded away.

Janis looked round curiously, smiling at Rachel who was staring at them with blank eyes.

'Hello,' she said but Benton turned away and started tidying a pile of wool.

Alan looked soberly at Violette but his eyes were quick and alive.

'We've come to rescue the wage slave,' he said.

'Yes,' Violette looked down at the counter.

'So what's this job you've got?' she asked without interest.

Her mother, still glowing, still happy, almost sang as she described the office, her boss, the other girls. 'I've gone back to legal work. Before you were born, I was a legal secretary. I enjoyed it. It was interesting work. Well, I've gone back to it now. It's such a challenge. And –' she laughed. 'Best of all, Saturdays off.'

'Oh, good.' Violette was miserably aware of tears at the back of her eyes.

'Yes, it is good, isn't it?'

The wool smelt sharper than ever. Alan leant closer to the girl. 'Are you all right this morning?' he asked gently.

She nodded, her face flaming as memories of the

previous night flooded back.

'The play wasn't that bad, was it?' Janis asked, misunderstanding.

Violette managed a whispered 'No,' and then, more strongly, 'No, really. It was me, making a fuss about going home.'

'Did you?' Janis was absent-minded. 'Oh, I don't recall that.'

'No reason why you should,' Alan put in.

Violette was glad Alan hadn't said anything to her mother. She hardly knew why she didn't want Janis to know. Once upon a time, in the old days, her mother would have been the first person she would have told. She stopped. Would she? Would she have admitted the attack to her mother? She was almost sure she would. Then she thought of all the women across the country. Would it be easier to talk to any one of them?

Her body still ached from the man's pressure. Her lips were sore from where she had rubbed and rubbed at them. She felt if she showered three times a day for the rest of her life, she would be no cleaner.

Janis touched her.

'You're miles away. Come on, get your coat. You look as if you could do with a break.'

Without even looking at Rachel, Violette knew she would be drinking it all in.

'Yes. I'm . . . I'm glad you've come,' she forced out, even managing a laugh. 'But can you wait a bit? Mrs Bartlett's gone out, but she shouldn't be long.'

'Well, we'll have a look around whilst we're waiting,' Janis said and Violette could have wept. She wanted her mother out of the shop, away from Benton's hostile prying eyes.

'I didn't mean wait in the shop.'

Her mother frowned.

'There might be something I want to buy. You carry on. We'll just look around.' She glanced at the shop clock. 'It's almost twelve. Your Mrs Bartlett shouldn't be long now.'

Rachel had moved to stand near them, watching, listening, until Janis, puzzled, asked, 'Was there something?'

The sharp words didn't make sense to Violette. 'Was there something?' and yet Rachel turned away instantly.

With a shrug and a look of amusement at Alan, Janis walked over to the materials. Alan moved towards Violette. She could see him coming. Two steps and he was there.

She took refuge behind the till, scribbling nonsense on a loose paper bag, pretending to be busy.

Alan watched her a moment, then placed a warm hand over hers, stopping her writing. For the life of her, she could not have moved but she didn't want this. Not yet.

'You two going to hold hands all day, then?' The hard voice broke through and for the first and only time in her life, Violette felt grateful to Benton. Grateful for the meanness of spirit which had prompted the remark. Alan moved his hand and stepped back from the counter.

Rudely, Benton elbowed Violette out of the way and rang up the money she was holding. She placed the notes in the till and slammed the drawer. Violette walked across to her mother. In the same instant, Mrs Bartlett burst through the shop door.

'I tried to get back sooner,' she called. 'I'm so sorry, girls.'

The clock showed five minutes past the hour.

'Well, what can you do?' the manageress appealed to Janis. 'It's my eyes. I never get time to go to the opticians' usually. Still,' she smiled on them all. 'Violette's a good girl. I can always trust her.'

Rachel made a sound as if she was being sick.

'Are you ill, my girl?' Mrs Bartlett asked, her voice sharp. 'I say to you, are you ill?'

Rachel shook her head.

'Then don't make such disgusting noises.'

Violette found she was grinning. She fetched her coat, walking past Benton and repeating quietly, 'I say to you, are you ill?' then laughed.

The morning had turned a little brighter.

She went to the restaurant along the street from the shop with Janis and Alan. They ate pizza and chips, drank coffee, considered gateau and cream, all without saying anything that couldn't be said in a crowded room. Janis ate and talked with a relaxed gaiety Violette had never seen in her before. She was obviously happy.

'You must come and see me,' she said now. Violette's leg jerked against Alan's.

Alan looked at her, surprised.

'Sorry,' Violette muttered. 'It was an accident.'

The young man shrugged, and half smiled.

Janis went on, 'You must come, Violette, now I've got my flat. Oh, it isn't much. It isn't all that good really, but it is mine.' She stopped, shy. She smiled again in a familiar sweet way and Violette wondered how she could ever have left them, this dear precious mother, how could she have gone? How could they have let her leave?

Alan's leg nudged, settled, moved slowly up and down against her leg. She thought everyone would hear the *rasp, rasp* of his leg against hers.

It was her turn to look at him. He grinned.

'Oh, sorry,' he said. 'An accident.'

'What's wrong with you two?' Janis demanded. 'I might as well talk to thin air as talk to you.' She tapped Violette's hand. 'Were you listening?'

'Aren't I always?'

Carefully, Violette picked up her fork and speared a piece of cold pizza.

'Then will you come and see me?' Janis pressed. 'Will you come tonight? There's so much to say and . . .' She smiled. 'On a lighter note, there's so much to show you.'

She stopped here and looked first at her daughter and then at Alan.

'Come this evening, right?'

Alan's restless fingers beat a tattoo on the table. As if making a sudden decision, he pressed his leg firmly against Violette's.

'That wasn't a mistake,' he said. 'There's no mistake about that.'

Janis looked from one to the other.

'I wish you two'd let me in on what's going on.'

All Violette wanted him to do was to move his leg. She breathed deeply, looking into the challenging blue eyes, then turned her attention back to her plate.

She picked up her fork and said to Janis, 'I'd like to come tonight but I can't. I can't come because I'm busy.'

Alan's leg nudged hers. He grinned.

Without pausing, Violette made to stab another chip, seemed to miss because of inattention and almost jumped out of her skin when the fork pierced the back of Alan's hand.

Before the young man could react, she had pulled the fork away and dropped it noisily onto the table.

'Godddd.' Alan breathed out on a long note of shock. 'For God's sake, Violette. I was only joking. What did you do that for?'

He closed his eyes briefly, his face pale and hurt.

Janis stared at him in alarm, her eyes going down to the marks on the back of his hand.

'What on earth?' Her startled voice sounded too loud.

Violette felt as if she was frozen to the moment. She had to make a huge effort to speak.

'I'm sorry.' She had no breath. 'Alan, I'm so sorry. I didn't mean to . . . ' She started to cry.

Violette felt she could hardly bear it. She knew in her heart Alan had been teasing her, that it had been a bit of fun but the dark things from last night had crowded her too soon and too heavily.

'I'm sorry. Please, please forgive me.'

She scrabbled for her handkerchief and dabbed at the little spots of blood. Four spots of blood in a row. As fast as she dabbed them away, they sprang back.

'I wasn't looking what I was doing.' Tears dripped off the end of her nose, poured down her face. 'The fork slipped.'

She realised this was the first time she had cried since the attack had happened but now she had started, she couldn't stop.

Alan sucked the back of his injured hand, turning his head away from the girl.

He spoke to Janis. 'I'll be getting along. There's a lot to see to this afternoon.'

'But . . .' Janis was bewildered. She gestured to Violette. 'It was an accident. She's so upset, Alan.'

'Yes,' he said. 'And so she should be.'

Violette could not stop the tears. Janis turned to her. 'It's all right, my love,' she comforted, alarmed by the increasing violence of the weeping. 'It's all right. It's not that bad. Just a few marks.'

Heads were turning as Violette wept on. She could hear herself. The incredible noise she was making. Sniffing, choking, gulping, almost howling.

'Get me out of here,' she wailed. 'Please.'

Her mother helped her out of the restaurant.

'Ah, shut up!' Alan flung at her when they were standing on the pavement. 'Just shut up.'

'Leave her,' Janis said, indignant. 'Don't talk to her like that.'

He was burning with anger against her. She could see it. Could see the mixture of pain and rage and hurt in his eyes.

Violette became aware that she was standing in the middle of a busy pavement, as alone as if she were a stranger to both her companions. No-one had their arms round her. No-one was wiping away her tears.

Still weeping, she turned from them and started to run back to the shop. She barged into people, sending them flying out of her way.

'You ought to look where you're going, you did.'

'Clumsy devil.'

At last, thankfully, she was at the side passage to the shop and she stepped into it.

She leant against the wall, wanting the rough brick to catch her face. Anything. Anything to feel different. To take her mind off what was in her head.

She heard steps. Steady, even steps walking down towards her. She let her head sink lower. She didn't care who it was. Then a hand touched her shoulder. Janis. This was coming to seem the only way they made physical contact these days. Her mother's hand on her shoulder. She shrugged it off.

'I'm all right,' she muttered before Janis had spoken. 'Leave me alone.'

'You always did say that,' Janis said, her voice warm and loving. 'My poor little Violette.'

She tugged gently on the girl's shoulder, slipping an arm around her but Violette found she didn't want her mother's concern. She pushed off the wall, away from her and turned to face Janis, scrubbing at her eyes with the backs of her hands.

'I'm OK. Honestly.'

'But what was all that about?' Janis asked curiously. 'All that in the restaurant. What was it about?'

'Nothing.' The girl shook her head. 'It was about nothing.'

Janis tried to hold the girl but Violette wanted none of it. Her head ached. She felt too that she was always crying when she saw her mother. This was the last time, she vowed it would be the last time.

'I'd better be getting back to work. I only get forty-five minutes. There's a lot to do.'

Janis nodded and finally let her go.

'If that's what you want.'

'That's what I want.'

As Violette looked at her mother, for a moment she longed to break down and tell her about the pain. But where would she start? She shrugged. Losing Janis? That would go down like a brick. The attack? She skated over this. Her worries about her Dad? Ho! Ho! Mark?

There was nowhere to start.

'I'm sorry about Alan's hand. I didn't mean to do it.'

She had control now.

'No, well . . .' The cool voice trailed away. 'Look, if you're sure you're OK, I'd better go.' Janis glanced at her watch. 'Lord, lord, look at the time. I'm late.'

'You go.' The girl reassured her. 'I was just . . . I dunno . . . anyway, it's gone now. You go.'

'Ring me,' her mother said, then turned and walked back down the gloomy passage.

Violette watched her go. She half thought Janis would turn and wave but she didn't. She quite understood. Life was all goodbyes.

It was dark where she stood so when the grey man who had been at the Social Club stepped into the opening from the street, she knew he couldn't see her. He stood there for quite some time, and Violette stood where she was, hardly breathing.

Then he was gone and she wondered what he was doing around Janis again.

She shivered. She must remember to mention it to someone. Who?

Just at that moment she couldn't think of anyone she could tell one living thing to.

Frowning, she turned and made her way back to the shop.

Chapter Eight

The only safe place in the world seemed to be her bedroom. Violette spent hours lying on her bed, listening to records, experimenting with make-up. She drifted in and out of school cutting most classes. Her work suffered. Mr Davies marked her books with increasing ferocity.

At last he tackled her.

'I don't know what's happened to you,' he said briefly. 'But I'll tell you one thing. There's no way you're going to pass your exams at this rate. You aren't doing enough work to support a flea, let alone a Hamlet.'

He gave a short laugh.

'Listen to this.'

He read aloud.

'Hamlet was a creation of William Shakespeare. Shakespeare seems to think he can do anything he likes with Hamlet. Well, I want to protest. I think Hamlet gets a raw deal. Writers should be shot.'

He flung the book on the table.

'That's not going to get you very far, Violette, especially –' he paused. 'Especially as the question set had absolutely nothing to do with the answer given.'

Violette looked out of the classroom window. The trees that fringed the playing fields looked like smudges of green paint.

'Are you listening?'

'I'm always listening,' she said.

Mr Davies fell silent, tapping his pen on the table top, noting the tiredness and dejection that flowed from the girl.

He had heard rumours, of course, about the parents. Separated. The mother had been seen with a younger man. Whatever had happened, it was affecting Violette. He wondered what he could do. Call in and see the father, perhaps. Ask the father to come up to school – or the mother. Take the whole matter to the Head.

He wasn't sure. Yet, it seemed hard to him that the girl's future should be put at risk because of what the parents were up to.

He made a decision.

'I'm going to give you another two weeks to pull yourself together. If there's no improvement, I shall have to put everything to the headmaster.'

Rachel had spread the story about Janis and Alan around the school. Violette scarcely bothered to speak to anyone. Even her closest friends found her forbidding and aloof. She knew she dared not be as she used to be. She was on guard all the time, waiting for sneering, unkind words. Waiting to be snubbed.

She trusted no-one, not even the people who had always been trustworthy and so she grew more and more isolated and alone.

Janis rang two or three times a week. There was nothing to talk about. After the incident in the restaurant, she hadn't repeated her invitation to Violette to see the flat, but then, just over a month later, she rang again.

'Come up tonight. I want to see you, Violette. I miss you. Mark's been. If he can make the effort, surely you can.'

'Why can't I be more like Mark?' Violette asked and

put the phone down.

It was all too much effort.

That evening was warm. She couldn't bear to be in the house so she walked out to the park. Down one road leading to the pit, tyres had been burnt. The pall of black smoke had been visible over the whole town. The smell sickened.

Violette thought of these wry, silent men fighting for their beliefs and she wondered how you got to that point. What made anyone care so much? She couldn't care about anything herself.

She thought of all the revolutions there had been in the world: all the protests, the death, the martyrdom – and for what? Why? How? Where did the men and women and children get their energy from? What fuelled it? Did their fiery blood shoot through their veins, pulse into their hearts, force their bodies on, without their consent?

It was all a complete mystery to her. She could almost see her energy draining away through the soles of her feet. She looked down at the grass, lifting a foot, as if she would really find a dark footprint beneath her.

Thoughtfully she stared at the Library. Why not? It looked fairly welcoming. She couldn't see anyone about and that was important. She didn't want to go where she could see people.

The bodies in the park blended with the grass and the trees and the slanting sun.

Up the steps, into the Library, over the polished floor.

The smell of the polish cheered her. The books on their shelves stood in neat rows. They would comfort her, she was sure they would.

She wandered over to the poetry, picking up Shakespeare's *Sonnets*.

Then hate me if thou wilt, if ever now.

Who needed it? She changed the book.

Sonnets from the Portuguese. Elizabeth Barratt Browning.

How do I love thee, let me count the ways.

An image of Alan flashed into her mind and it was so clear, so dazzling, she had to grab the side of the shelf to support herself.

How do I love thee, let me count the ways.

She thought now of her mother, with her passionate bid for freedom. No, she didn't want to call Janis 'mother'. Who wanted to call a passionate woman 'mother'?

She put the books back on the shelf. She had to get out. What had make her think books would give her anything? Deliberately she banged against a carousel of paperbacks and the whole thing fell over with a huge clatter. Books spilt everywhere. Books went flying across the polished floor, skidding under the checking-out counter, sliding the length of a librarian's foot.

Violette looked at the librarian. She was glad she'd done that. Glad she'd released the books. Happy books.

She left them where they were and walked on, shoulders hunched.

The librarian stared after her. These girls, she thought with exasperation. These young teenage girls. The things they carried around with them! She wondered if they knew. They were like flame throwers, devastating whole areas before them, around them, behind them.

She looked at the spilt books.

'Kids,' she said furiously, and bent to pick them up.

In the park, Violette wandered to a seat. The wood was warm from the sun, so she sat down, touching it with her hand. The sun shadowed as a body lowered beside her.

She started to rise but a hand drew her back.

'It's only me,' Alan said. 'Don't go.'

Violette could hardly believe she hadn't been aware of

his presence in the park. Hadn't known he was approaching her. She had thought she would always know when he was around.

She kept her eyes fixed firmly on the ground.

Slowly, an enormous mound of snow white bandages crept into her view.

She stared at them. One solitary finger tip waggled. That was the only flesh she could see.

She looked up at Alan in dismay.

'Did I do that to you?'

Gingerly, she took hold of the hand.

'Ouch!' he winced. 'Be careful. Watch what you're doing. They were saying I might have to have it off.'

She was shattered.

'Have it off?' she repeated. 'What, the whole hand?'

Alan rocked with laughter.

'Your face!' he said. 'You should see your face.'

She took him in, the merry eyes, the laughing open face, the lovely straight firm lips.

'Were you kidding?' she started, beginning to smile despite herself.

'It's got to come off,' he wailed with laughter. 'The whole hand. Off. Off with his head as well.'

She watched in amazement as he toppled slowly off the bench and lay prostrate on the grass. He reached a hand out to her and she took it. Took the strong young hand so that he pulled her down to him.

'Laugh,' he ordered. 'Laugh.'

And she laughed.

The park was empty. Alan lifted his body up and leaned over her. She was still laughing. In the last fling of sunshine which lit his face and outlined his body in a glowing golden light, his face was inches above hers.

She slid out from beneath him and sat up. Alan flung

himself back on his elbow, picking at the dry grass, watching her.

'Let me look at that hand,' she demanded and he lifted the bandaged hand to her.

She unwrapped the bandage. There was miles of it. The breeze caught it and whipped it along the grass and still it unfurled.

'How much have you used?' she asked, astonished.

'A bit.'

She came to the end of the bandage at last and let it go. The wind picked it up and trailed it over the grass and into the rose beds. The long strip of white twisted and turned among the leaves and flowers.

'Vandal,' Alan remarked. 'Litter lout.'

She examined the back of his injured hand. There were four tiny marks.

'It isn't even bleeding.'

'It isn't now, but it was.'

She ran her finger over the marks then, impulsively, put the hand to her lips.

He watched her, heavy eyed.

Without speaking, she sucked at the four tiny marks. He let her, neither drawing close to her nor pulling away.

'How old are you?' he asked.

She let his hand drop. He didn't seem bothered.

'Sixteen.'

'Still at school?'

'Only because I want to be.'

'You're staying on?'

She nodded.

'Janis was married when she was eighteen months older than I am.'

He grew thoughtful.

'I miss her,' she went on. 'Since she left home, I really

miss her.'

'Home isn't what she wants any more,' Alan said and Violette nodded again.

'I know. I know it isn't.' She paused, then went on painfully. 'My mother has remade herself.' She didn't care whether he understood her or not. 'She just decided one day she didn't want what she'd got, so she left it all behind her. She picked a row with my Dad . . .' another hesitation. 'In a way I wish she'd been more honest. Just come straight out with it. You know, why she was leaving and everything. Just sort of said it was because she wanted to be somebody different. This way, she's left us all thinking it's our fault.'

'It all boils down to choices,' Alan murmured. 'I suppose your mother thought she'd served her time.'

Violette turned to him.

'Is that how it seems?' she asked, puzzled. 'That she'd "served her time"? It's as if she thought of it all . . . all of it . . . me, Mark, my Dad . . . as a prison sentence.'

'It can be, to some people.'

'Then why marry?'

'Oh well, as to why marry, why ask? People are different at eighteen to thirty eight. Their needs change, their desires alter.'

She glanced at him on the word 'desires'.

'Yes,' she said. 'Yes.' She moved restlessly on the grass. 'She reminds me of Shakespeare.'

Alan laughed.

'I didn't know she was a writer.'

'She isn't. Not a "words on pages" writer, anyway. She . . . she has created a new character, though. She's a new character. Shakespeare does that all the time, invents new characters just so he can destroy them. I don't think he liked people very much.'

'Do you have to?'

She shook her head.

'I don't suppose so. Janis didn't like her old self, did she? That's why she destroyed her and made a whole new person to put in the old skin.' She played with a blade of grass. 'You can't settle for that, though, can you? You have to have new people around you as well, so that you can keep the new person going. So that they'll treat you as a new person. That's where me and Mark and my Dad fall down, we're just the same old people. We can't be new for this new Janis. We couldn't treat her as somebody new in our lives.' She hesitated. 'Honest. I just don't see how we could.'

'Come on.' Alan scrambled to his feet. 'Let's walk.'

They walked around the park, through the patches of wild grass and under the trees. Alan put an arm lightly round her shoulders. It was nice. Comfortable. She was glad now that she'd come out.

'What were you doing here?' she asked as they walked through the iron gates and into the street.

'Looking for you.'

They walked in silence.

'I called at your house. Your Dad said you'd headed towards the Library.'

They stopped opposite the old Priory.

'Do you want to go in?'

Violette didn't know if she wanted to go in.

'Come on. It'll be interesting.'

'I've seen it so many times.'

'But not with me.'

They stared at the serene building in front of them.

'I don't understand about energy,' she said now. 'Where they get it from. These people. People who're committed. Like Janis. Like the people who built this.' She made a vague gesture. She turned to face him. 'I don't have that 'kind of energy.'

'That might be a good thing,' Alan said drily. 'Energy has to be spent, Violette. Any kind of energy. You can't pile it up inside because if you do, it explodes. Destroys you. You have to act. Energy comes with commitment but commitment means action. Your mother found commitment to a Cause so she acted.'

'Yes, well, her very first Cause was us and her very first commitment used to be her family.'

'There are impersonal Causes,' he pointed out. 'Where the person isn't the primary consideration.'

'But what about our family? Don't we count either?'

'What is a family?' He returned the word to her with great kindness. 'What is a family when each individual member is old enough to look after themselves?'

They went into the Church, the great doors opening before them. In the tiny Lady Chapel, communicants were kneeling at the altar. Violette wondered if the rough stone dug into their knees.

They sat in the body of the Church on the wooden chairs ranked for a Service.

Alan looked round the deep shadowed building.

'Monks used to walk here. Can you imagine them, Violette? I bet they loved it. I bet their whole lives were swept along in this community.'

He thought about the monks. About the deep unending passion of religious faith. About the rivalries, the loyalties, the heady excitements of church politics.

Communion ended. People drifted out of the Lady Chapel and Violette turned to watch them go, struck by their quietness.

At the farther reaches of the Church, at the end of one of the rows, was the grey man from the South Elms Social Club. She couldn't take her eyes off him and he in turn stared levelly back at her.

She nudged Alan.

'There's a man at the back who was in the Club,' she said. 'And I saw him outside the shop.'

Alan stiffened.

'How do you know he was in the Club?' he asked without lifting his head.

'Because he was sat at the side of me. And he was watching Janis. And the last time I saw him, outside the shop, I think he was watching Janis then as well.'

She remembered again the way the grey man had stared at her mother.

'Who is he? Do you know?'

The young man coughed.

'I'm not totally sure who he is but my guess would be that he's probably Special Branch.'

'You've got to be kidding,' Violette said. 'This isn't the telly, you know. This is here.'

'But this isn't *just* here,' he corrected her. 'It's here during the Miner's Strike. You can't have missed what's happening in the town?'

'Don't be so bloody patronising,' the girl flared. 'Do you think I'm blind? Do you think Janis left home to start a day nursery? Don't patronise me. I'm paying for this Strike just the same as everybody else.'

Alan took a deep breath.

'Sorry,' he said.

They sat together, waiting.

'He's probably Special Branch,' Alan enlarged, 'because there's too much activity around here. They like to keep tabs on people.'

'Who's he keeping tabs on then?'

'You?' Alan grinned. 'Or me?'

'You,' Violette confirmed. 'It's you –' and then, '– and

Janis, isn't it? You and Janis.'

He nodded.

'Yes,' he said. 'It's all of us. All of us.'

'Well, what are you doing? What are you doing that makes you so interesting?'

He drew away from her, surprised.

'I thought you knew,' he said. 'I'm a Union man.'

There was no sound at all in the Church, yet Violette could see a black robed Priest moving around. Into the Lady Chapel. Out of the Lady Chapel.

Alan sighed.

'Don't you understand anything?' he asked, impatience edging his voice. 'Why do you think the police walk around in pairs? Why don't they have numbers on their uniforms? How many men and women have been hurt and arrested? What happens to them when they're in the Police Stations? Do you want to know the time?'

He laughed, a harsh bitter sound. 'Does this place make you feel holy? Does it make you feel anything?'

She was stubborn.

'It doesn't make me feel anything at all.'

He seemed not to hear her.

'You know my politics. They stem from here. From the things you're taught in these places. "All men are equal,"' he quoted.

'But some are more equal than others,' Violette finished.

'And some are too bloody clever by half.'

Violette flushed.

She turned to look for the grey man again. The Church was empty.

'He's gone, Alan.'

'He won't have gone far.'

'Let us go.'

She saw how tired he was.

'None of it should have happened,' he muttered. 'It's the way they treat you. As if you're not a human being. It's the contempt that gets you. You reach a point where you think you'll knock that off their faces if it kills you and sod the consequences.'

He returned again and again to the same refrain.

'You have to have respect. Without respect, where are you? You might as well be a pig in a sty.'

She touched his face.

'Come on. Let's go.'

They were silent, walking down the wide centre aisle. Alan held her hand.

'I'll be glad when it's all over,' she said at last.

'Yes,' he agreed. 'I suppose you will.'

Gladness. Yes, he remembered gladness.

'Oh, come on,' he seized her arm. 'Let's get out of here.'

They grinned at each other, brought alive in an instant. His fingers on her arm, her skin under his hand brought them alive. They ran down the rest of the aisle, their noisy feet banging sound into the silence. They tumbled through the big doors and out into the paved court beyond.

They ran without stopping all the way back to the gates of the Library.

'I can't go any further,' Violette gasped. 'I've got stitch.'

They sank, laughing, onto the little stone wall. Alan pulled her to him.

He smiled, a great open smile.

'You come to me,' he whispered. 'You just come to me,' and she went to him, half unwillingly.

He kissed her and she sensed his drowning in her. Alan closed his eyes to the trees, to the park, to the people around them, drawing from the girl what he wanted, what he needed.

Violette felt such a force of feeling, she found it difficult not to shake. His lips on her were hard. They demanded a response. She closed her eyes in submission to that demand and then opened them to hold reality to her. She could see Alan's grainy skin. His eyelids flickered. She glimpsed the blue unseeing eyes and they made her burn and tremble.

Chapter Nine

When Violette reached home, the house had settled down for the evening. Alan had left her without arranging a further meeting. The hall was shadowed and quiet as she opened the door. She slipped her coat off and, without pausing, started for the stairs. She wanted time to think about Alan and about all that had passed between then.

'Is that you?' a voice called and reluctantly, the girl hesitated.

'I thought I heard you,' her father said, opening the middle door and staring out at her. 'Don't go upstairs. Your mother's here. She wants to see you.'

'Here? What – in the house?'

'That's what I said. Come on. I've got to make the tea so you might as well entertain her while I do.'

Violette was slow to move, not wanting to see her mother and not wanting the thoughts in her head to spoil.

'Have I got to?'

'Don't be ridiculous,' her Dad snapped. 'Of course you've got to.'

It was as she was moving across the hall that a sudden image slipped into her mind. Janis and Alan together. She stopped, confused. Had Alan called at the house with her mother? No. Her mind pulled away from that. Had he been sent to find her? Is that why he'd turned up in the

Park? She felt the blood rushing into her face. And she'd been so glad to see him. Wait. Wait. What if he had been with her mother? So what? What did it matter? A kiss. What was a kiss between friends?

Oh, blow the lot of them. She could manage without anyone. She scowled. One thing was for sure. She was certainly learning how to.

'Come on, dreamer,' her Dad tapped her as he passed. 'Just go in and see your Mum and stop worrying. You look as if you've lost a pound and found a penny.'

Violette thought that was a good description of how she felt.

She sighed. So what, so what, so what.

She opened the door to the room. Her mother sat looking out of the window, the golden wing of her hair shining in the soft lamplight.

Violette stood a moment and watched her, noting the curve of her cheek, the attempt she was making to appear relaxed, when her legs and feet were taut against each other.

'Mother,' she said, knowing there must be a moratorium on being woman to woman whilst they were in the house. After all, this was the house she had been born in. How could Janis not acknowledge her motherhood when she had first become a mother in the room above?

Janis turned. Violette was taken aback. Her mother looked . . . what was it? She couldn't find the word. And then Violette knew the word. Sensual. That was it. There was a radiance, a deep aliveness about Janis. She wondered if she had always had that radiance. That sensuality. She guessed she must have. After all, her Dad had married her. Had Alan . . . she stopped.

Why could she see it now? Why now – when she didn't want to see it, acknowledge it, be aware of it?

The girl closed her eyes briefly but when she opened them, it seemed to her that Janis, hazy and voluptuous, was in the centre of a storm of pollen. Violette wouldn't have been at all surprised if a swarm of bees had flown into the room, sleek and soft, to nibble at her mother with their black feelers, coveting and seizing the rich dust she was sure had settled on the creamy skin.

She felt positive now that Alan had been with her mother. Positive that he had put that downy creamy look onto and into Janis. Positive that her mother was reflecting experiences lived out of sight of family, out of sight of any relationship that trespassed on her own self.

Her mother spoke.

'I wanted to see you, Violette. You obviously weren't going to come to me so I've come to you. I wanted to make sure you were OK.'

Well, none of this made sense.

'What do you mean? OK? Why shouldn't I be OK?'

The hostility stopped her mother. There was a short tense pause then Janis started again.

'I wasn't happy when I left you last time. I don't know what was going on between you and Alan but there was something. It isn't that I mind so much but what I do mind is that it got in the way of you and me and it's staying in the way.'

Violette looked out of the window.

'Violette, look, somehow, you and I have to work things out between us.'

'Why?'

Her mother was silent for a minute or two. Her voice was low when she began to speak.

'Don't tell me you're not bothered about us, Violette? Don't tell me you're prepared to let sixteen years of loving and living with each other go down the drain because you can't be bothered to come and see me, to come and talk to me?'

'What is there to talk about?'

Janis bent her head. Violette thought her mother looked more delicate than she used to. Well, let her.

'Please don't let's argue.' Janis tried again. 'I don't want to argue. That's the very last thing I want to do but I can't do everything on my own. You've got to meet me halfway.'

'You've done everything on your own so far.'

'I have not. I never wanted there to be this estrangement between us, Violette. I truly thought we could work out a new and more honest relationship. I still believe that. I still want to try.'

Violette couldn't think of anything to say.

'I'm having a party tomorrow night . . .'

The girl laughed.

'A party.'

'Yes, a party. What's wrong with that? I want you to come to it. Please.'

Violette turned away from her mother's eyes.

'I don't like parties.'

'Then come before it starts so that we can talk.'

'Will Alan be there?'

Janis frowned, little lines marking her forehead.

'I expect so. Yes, I should think he will be there.'

'Oh, I dunno. I'll see what I feel like.'

Janis stared at her.

'Would you give that kind of answer to anyone else, Violette?' She went on, 'I mean, if one of your friends . . .'

'I haven't got any friends.'

'If one of your friends asked you to a party, is that what you'd say? "I'll see what I feel like"?'

Violette shrugged.

'So OK, I'll come.'

Janis felt exhausted, as if she had run a race where the finishing line was kept secret.

'Are you ever coming back?' Violette asked with grim stubbornness. 'Are you and Dad ever going to get back together?'

Janis hardly seemed to have heard her. She was looking round the room and without even being aware of it, she shivered with distaste. Violette could see it written on her face. Everything in the room was horrible to Janis. Even the things she had chosen herself.

Violette let her own eyes wander round. She used to dislike most of the things. She had always hated the vases, the carpet, the curtains – but now she wasn't so sure. She thought she might like the room. Yes, she thought she just might.

'Will it contaminate you?' she asked now.

Janis bit her lip.

'I'm sorry. It's just . . . oh, I don't know what it is. Perhaps you grow out . . .'

'And you talk about *my* manners,' Violette put in.

'I'm sorry.'

'You should finish what you were saying. Perhaps you grow out of people as well as things.'

Before her mother could reply, her Dad was back, handing out cups of tea and ginger biscuits.

Violette looked from one to the other. She wondered how long her mother had been in the house. Whilst she was there, Violette had been in the park, in the Church. She could hear Alan's voice, feel the stone beneath her feet, see his fierce face.

They were an untidy, unfriendly group sitting in the quiet room. Janis said little.

'Are you coping, then?' Peter asked at last, as if he had no interest either way.

His wife nodded.

'Do you have enough money?'

Janis waved a hand, as if even to think of money was a burden.

'I've got all I need.'

'You're both being very polite,' Violette said loudly. 'It must be nice to be polite. I'm not polite. My mother told me so. But you're polite, you two, you're very polite.'

They both looked at her, wary. She thought they were like animals who have been discovered in their lair. She hated them both.

'All this being polite. What's going on? Are we supposed to pretend nothing's happened? That there's nothing wrong. Be polite. Polite. Polite. Polite!' she screamed. 'Is that what we have to do. Be polite?'

Mark appeared in the doorway.

'You shouting again?' he said. 'You're always shouting. You're worse than them.'

There was a dark coldness in his voice that stopped his sister.

Mark lifted a finger and jabbed the air.

'You don't know what you're talking about, Violette. Didn't you know they've both got other people? That's why they're being polite. She isn't coming back here. Her. She's got somebody else and so has he. Oh, don't tell me you didn't know?' He grinned at the shock on Violette's face. 'If you didn't know that, well. You can't keep on being surprised. They don't care about us, about what we want. It's easier for them not to care. Easier for them to be polite. I can tell you this, you could talk to them until the cows came home and they wouldn't ever, ever get back together.'

His hand fell to his side.

'Well, that'll just do!' His Dad jumped up. 'That will

just do. You don't know what you're talking about, you, but that doesn't stop you, does it? I haven't got anybody else and neither has your mother.'

'Neither has your mother,' Mark mimicked.

'You stop that.' His Dad was furious. 'You two don't even begin to understand our problems. You don't even begin to understand and as far as I can see, you're neither of you, neither of you interested in understanding.'

Violette wondered if there was such a thing as understanding. Perhaps it was a catch word – a pit – a trap people fell into, shouting all the time that they wanted to be understood, to understand and really, there was no such thing as understanding.

Was understanding the same as approval, she wondered. Did you understand if you approved and not understand if you disapproved?

'Oh, stop shouting, Dad,' she said wearily.

'Don't you talk to me like that, young woman. Just remember who you're talking to, that's all.'

'Why don't you go?' Violette turned to her mother.

'And don't you talk to your mother like that either.'

'My mother?' Violette was incredulous. 'My mother? You've got to be kidding. You mistake things if you think Janis wants to be my mother. Huh, you could hardly be more wrong.'

'It isn't like that, Violette,' Janis protested. 'I do not not want to be your mother. I have no choice in that and neither do you. I am your mother and you are my daughter but for God's sake, you're old enough to see, surely, you're old enough to um . . . comprehend the need I have for some freedom of my own. Surely?' she appealed. 'What harm have I ever done you that you should turn against . . . judge . . . be as you are with me? I still want to be in your life. That's what this is all about. I never want you to move away from me so that I don't see you. So that there is no warmth and no closeness. All I want, all I have ever wanted is a little bit of freedom. Just to be free. Is it too much to ask? Is it?'

'Ten "I's".'

'What?'

'Ten "I's",' Violette repeated. 'In that speech.'

Janis stood up.

'I'd . . .' she stopped. 'I'd better go. It's hopeless talking to you. You've made up your mind about things and you won't change it. There's no room for change in you, Violette.'

This struck Violette as so unfair, she had no idea what to say. Before she could say anything, Mark snorted, a loud rude sound that made Peter instinctively clip the boy around the head. Mark hit back at his father. His fist caught Peter on the eye.

For a moment, no-one moved. Then Mark stood and yelled, his mouth wide open and the noise going on and on so that Violette felt as if there was nothing in the room but noise.

'Stop it! Stop it!' his Dad shouted. 'Get up to your room. Go on. Go on.' He tried to push the boy but Mark shoved him away and banged out through the door.

They all heard him run across the hall, the front door slamming behind him.

'It was a mistake coming back,' Janis whispered. 'I should have stayed away.'

'Yes, you should.' Violette was grief stricken. 'You should have stayed away. We don't want you here. You don't care about us. You don't care about Mark . . . you don't . . .'

It was too much trouble to go on.

'Hold on. You just hold on,' Janis came back at her. 'I'm

not the only relative Mark has standing in this room. You're his sister. If I'm so bad, so rotten as you keep saying I am, I'm surprised you want me to go after him, to care about him or about you. You take over, Violette. You care and you be seen to care. Just stop expecting me to be this perfect creature. This mother who lives only for her children. I can't do it, not any more. I just can't do it.' Her voice broke. 'But if you want to try, go ahead, don't let me stop you. Let's see what you make of it all.'

'He doesn't want me. I'm only his sister. He wants you. You're supposed to care about him.'

'I do care about him. I do care about you. I've spent a lifetime caring about you both. I've watched you grow up, helped you with your homework, fought for you, sided with you, loved you. I thought there was enough love, enough caring between us to see us over any trouble, and yet the first time I . . . the first time I step out of my frame, there's nothing for me. Nothing –' she paused. 'It would have been all the same if I had neglected you, not loved you, not cared, wouldn't it? I wouldn't have got anything then just as I'm not getting anything now.'

Janis picked up her bag and turned to the door.

'How can you say that?' Violette stormed. 'When it's all here for you?'

'Yes, here, as long as I stay here but I'm not here and I'm not staying here so just exactly what kind of love is on offer?'

'The same kind you're offering us,' Violette retorted bleakly. 'Exactly the same kind. Mother.'

'Violette, please. Please,' Janis pleaded. 'Try and see me in my own right – as a woman. I am a *woman*,' she insisted. 'I didn't spring from the womb with "Mother" tattooed on my forehead. I had to learn. We all have to learn. You'll have to learn. But those years are gone. I'm *me* now and

I'm going to keep on being me. I haven't let you down. I wanted a different relationship, that's all. I wanted you to see me as a friend, not just as a bloody mother all the time.'

Janis started to cry.

'I wanted a more honest, truer relationship where I didn't have to lie any more. I don't know. God, I just don't know. Why is it all so difficult? Why can't you . . .' her words trailed away and she pulled at the handle to the door.

Peter walked across.

'Look,' he said. 'This has to stop. We're a family.' He held a hand up. 'No, Violette. We are a family. It's just that your mother isn't living with us, that's all.'

'I spit on that,' Violette returned and her mother left without another word.

She and her father listened to yet another door closing.

Her father sighed.

'You managed to make a good mess of that,' he said but Violette shook her head.

'Who's this fancy woman of yours, then?'

She felt nothing. Nothing.

'You mind your tongue,' her Dad replied. 'There's no fancy woman, no woman at all. Mark saw me with a friend.'

'Whoah! A friend. Ha!'

'Watch it, Violette.'

There was nothing else to say. Violette looked at the time. 'I'm going after Mark.'

Her father turned away from her without answering.

The streets were crowded with young people out for the night. To Violette they all looked happy and carefree. She thought how good it must be to feel like that. Happy. Carefree. She wandered round and round the town but Mark was nowhere to be seen.

All the time she walked, her mother's words clattered in

her head. The longer the words went on, the more she felt as if she had been to a funeral. It was only when the wind got up that she realised she was very cold.

'I shall lose her,' she said aloud, trying it out for size. 'I shall lose her.'

She tried to imagine a world without her mother and knew that for her, for a long time, for ever, it would be a world in the shade. An unthinkable world.

Janis's words came back and back. 'I wanted you to see me as a friend, not just as a bloody mother all the time.' 'I'm a woman.'

The thought occurred to her that Alan respected her mother. She stood still. He did. She knew he did. Whatever else was between them, that much was true. He thought well of Janis.

She stopped in front of a dress shop and stared blindly into the window. Blacks and whites, that was all she could see, except for one splash of colour. A flower thrown on the floor.

'My world should be that straightforward,' she mumbled.

She thought then of where Mark would be and that was where she found him, playing the fruit machines.

She tapped him on the shoulder.

'Come on. You're coming home with me.'

He started to push her away.

'Keep your hands to yourself,' Violette warned, close to breaking. 'Just keep your hands to yourself.'

Mark saw the misery in her eyes and, grabbing her arm, propelled her out of the Arcade.

They marched home like tin soldiers, moving stiffly through the streets. Mark swore all the way back to the house, scarcely drawing breath except for more and more swearing.

Violette heard his voice going on and on. She patted his arm. Put her arm through his and pulled him close. Gradually, the voice steadied and quietened but the boy didn't fall silent until they were at their own front door.

Their father was in the kitchen, making a pot of tea. He seemed very tired. He looked up as his son marched in.

'You look done in. Come on, sit down and I'll make some toast.'

Violette thought she must be invisible.

'You, too,' her Dad said.

Mark started to talk and the words seemed almost to tear him apart.

'Shut up and eat.'

Her father's words penetrated. She ate too. The food warmed them both and quietened Mark.

'What's wrong?' her Dad asked, sensing a difference in the girl's anxiety. 'Tell me, Violette. Let me help.'

'There's nothing wrong, Dad.' She wanted to escape. 'Look, I'll go and make a fresh pot of tea.'

She made the tea, losing herself in the pictures in her mind. The Church. The Park. Alan. His kiss. Janis. They turned over, rolling and turning in her mind, over and over.

'A new day tomorrow,' her Dad murmured. 'A new beginning.'

Not for many, Violette thought suddenly. For many it would be just a continuance of today and the day before and the day before that. There couldn't always be a new start.

She was exhausted with her thoughts but one thing she settled on. She would go to Janis's party. Violette wanted to see where her mother lived, see how she lived, see if there was any place for her in Janis's new life.

This surprised her. Did she want a place in her mother's

new life? Cautiously, she nodded her head. Yes, she thought she did.

She hoped her mother was living in misery, really, so that she could feel sorry for her. If she felt sorry enough, she was almost sure she would wipe out all the things Janis had done. All the terrible wrongs her mother had done to them all.

Lifting the tea cup, sipping the hot liquid, Violette thought about the flat. There would be a room, a kitchen, a bathroom and yes, there would be a bedroom.

A vivid image of her mother and Alan twisting and turning on the bed sprang into her mind. She felt sick and pushed the thought away. Not her mother, not on a bed, limb to limb with Alan. It was terrible to think of her mother in that way. Wicked.

But she was a woman, wasn't she? She'd said so. 'I am a woman' and that's what women did.

But now, she herself was a young woman. A dart of hope came into her heart. Perhaps there was a way forward then, after all. Perhaps two women would find that they had things in common that a woman and a girl did not. Perhaps she and Janis could make a new start, could have a new beginning just as her Dad said.

And what if they failed? What then?

She wished that her mother had eaten hot toast and drunk tea with them.

Later, standing in her room, ready for bed, Violette pulled back the curtains and stared at the night. The moon was high. The trees across the road were black, each individual leaf a little black silken banner blowing in the night air.

She decided afresh. Tomorrow night she would go to her mother's party and there, with a bit of luck, she would see Alan.

They were both women so they started equal.

A cloud crossed the moon and the whole street darkened. Endings and beginning were lost in the shadows. Violette yawned. Tomorrow was another day.

Chapter Ten

It seemed silly afterwards, thinking Janis might be living in misery. The room Violette found herself in on the following evening was warm and well-lit. The girl stared at the furnishings – what there was of them.

'Are you surprised?' Janis asked, watching her daughter's eyes wander over the black chairs, the painted floor, the single painting on the wall, the wooden shutters against the window. There was nothing of home or comfort, Violette thought. You could walk in and walk out and the room wouldn't look any different.

'No, I'm not surprised,' she answered. 'I suppose if I'd stopped to think about it, this would be the kind of room you would have.'

Janis frowned. There was something different about Violette's voice. Violette, too, felt uneasy. There was a new element creeping into her feelings about her mother. She wasn't sure what it was but she felt that since Janis had forced her to reassess their relationship, she was finding there were things about her mother she didn't like.

She brooded about this. No, it wasn't the usual dislike that she felt all daughters felt for their mother at times. Impatience with rules. Dislike of this or that or the other because now, when she looked back, all her petty dislikes of Janis had been in some way connected with herself.

She had liked or disliked Janis only in as much as Janis had affected her at any particular time. It was becoming clear to Violette that she had never judged Janis as a person: that is, someone separate from herself.

'Come and meet everyone,' Janis urged. 'Later, when they've all gone, we'll have that talk.'

She held onto her daughter's hand and led her into the room. A whirl of introductions followed. Violette recognised many of the women from the play and from the early days of the strike.

There were a few men there, husbands, boy friends. Violette searched for Alan and then saw him, coming from another room.

'The bedroom,' her mind said clearly. 'He's come out of the bedroom.'

He saw her and threaded his way through the crush of people. Before he could reach her, other people laid claim to him. He raised his eyes and grimaced.

She couldn't smile, not to save her life, and as he looked at her not smiling, his keen young face softened. When he smiled again, it was a gentle rueful grin and this time she responded to it.

For a large part of the night, Alan was taken up with other people, other men and women, and, Violette noticed, other girls. He was a popular figure.

He finally made it to her side balancing two cups of coffee and two plates of pizza.

'Come on, Violette. Find a quiet place. I've got us some grub.'

They found a corner where no-one was sitting and Violette took the coffee from him as he sank down onto the carpet.

'You take the chair,' Alan grinned.

Violette sat down and took a plate from him. She looked

at the pizza then glanced up to find him watching her, a wry smile tugging at his lips.

'No fork this time,' he murmured and then, as she coloured, went on quickly, 'I'm sorry. I was teasing. I shouldn't.'

She could think of nothing to say. They ate in silence, as if that corner had a plate of glass between it and the room. She was so aware of him. Of everything he did.

As they ate, Violette felt a growing dismay. The food was almost finished, the coffee almost drunk and still they had barely exchanged a word. Before she could speak, a girl swayed up to them and held her hand out to Alan.

'Come on, Alan,' she tempted him. 'Come and dance. You like this number.'

The young man shook his head, laughing.

'No. You go and get someone else, Michelle. You're a slave driver, you are. I'm having a rest.'

The girl persisted.

'No,' she bent down to him. 'You come. I don't want anyone else. I want you. You're not doing anything. This is a party,' she emphasised. 'It's all right to have a good time. You're supposed to.'

'Michelle,' Alan started. 'Honest. I really don't feel like it just now.'

The girl's laughing face darkened. She made a mock frown.

'It would do you good,' she promised, eyes dancing, teeth glinting as she coaxed him.

Violette looked at the uncarpeted floor.

'You should go,' she muttered and he turned to her instantly.

'You can speak then.'

He waited for her reply, inclining his head to her, so close that if she had dared, she could have put her lips on his with only the smallest effort.

Michelle stood up, putting her hands on her hips.

'Remember me?' she said. 'What am I? Invisible or something?'

Alan got to his feet. He put an arm around Michelle and led her across the room, talking to her the whole time, laughing down into the girl's smiling face.

Violette found her lips were shaking. She felt unbearably hot. Why had she told him to go when she didn't want him to? Well, that was a lesson learned, wasn't it? She should be more careful. But no, she knew she would never be more careful. She was angry with herself. It wasn't in her to be more careful, was it? And then, astonishingly, Alan was back and now it was his turn to lean down to her, his turn for his smiling coaxing face to tempt her onto the floor.

'Come on, sour puss. Come and dance.'

Violette hesitated between taking offence or going with the swirl of joy that shot through her.

With a grin, she stood up.

'I thought you'd never ask,' she said and over his shoulder she could see Michelle staring at them both.

Now the record changed and a funny fast melody poured into the room. Violette felt high. She could almost hear her mother saying, 'Have you been drinking?' just as she used to when she had felt that way in the past.

Alan felt it. He felt her gaiety, her sparkling, shining mood. It was contagious. He moved to her and they started to dance.

As the music went on, they both grew more happy, more innovative. Other people stopped dancing to watch them, cheering them on.

'Cha Cha Cha!' Alan roared.

'Olé!' Violette shouted back.

They were giddy with joy. In and out, round and round, touching and moving away, holding and loosening the hold, breast to breast, arm to arm, leg to leg, on they went until with a final flourish, the music ended and Violette, blazing with life, struck a last pose, both arms stretched upwards, her head dropping back so that her hair swung free. Alan put his arm round her waist and twirled her round the room.

The watching people applauded. It was good to see such brightness in the middle of the dark times they were involved in.

Laughing and breathless, Alan and Violette came to a halt.

'That was good,' Alan said and bent to kiss her.

She kissed him back, wanting only for his lips to stay on hers, wanting the kiss to go on for ever. In the middle of her exhausted happiness, she felt a sharp stab of desire for him. The strength of it caught her by surprise and, taken aback, she pushed him away.

Alan laughed, punching the air with his fist.

He turned to her.

'You're wet through with sweat.'

He drew his hand across her forehead, sliding his fingers down her face and over the damp bow of her lips.

Then, Michelle was back, pulling at his shirt.

'You promised me the next dance and here it is,' she said.

'Go on,' Violette urged. 'You go and dance. I need to cool down.'

She watched as they started to dance in the middle of the room. It was a slow number. Michelle's arms crept around Alan's body. Violette turned away.

'He's enjoying himself.'

Her mother stood with her.

'Are you enjoying yourself?' Janis pressed on.

Violette glanced at her. Janis was watching the dancers. She seemed distracted.

'It's a good party,' Violette offered but Janis moved away without reply.

There was no opportunity for her to dance with Alan again. As soon as Michelle released him, Janis was in Alan's arms and Violette thought sourly that where Alan was, her mother was always close by.

Janis, Michelle, Violette, the girl turned the names over in her head. Who else was there?

The joy had gone. Now she couldn't imagine it had ever been there. Couldn't imagine where it had sprung from. How stupid she was. The first thing she had seen coming into her mother's was Alan coming out of the bedroom. You couldn't get away from that. And then Michelle. So. Really, she dismissed Michelle. She wished she could dismiss her mother as easily.

Then, all at once it seemed, it was last cups of coffee and the guests went out into the night.

Standing with her mother on the doorstep, Violette shivered.

'I think I'd better go as well,' she said but Janis wouldn't hear of it.

'You can't go now,' she protested. 'We haven't had chance to talk. There's plenty of time. Your Dad knows where you are. It won't matter if you're late back for once. If you're worried, I'll ring him. Tell him.'

'No, don't do that. I'd really rather go home. Let's leave the talking to another night.'

Violette felt bored with the idea of talking to her mother. It would be like breaking concrete, she knew it would. She flinched at the thought of more pain, more probing. Surely it was better now to let skin form over the sores, instead of

121

poking and prodding at them.

'I just want to leave it,' she said again.

Janis was tired. She yawned, stretching her arms and Violette was reminded of that terrible night at the South Elms Social Club. She could see her mother now, stretching, stretching, and Alan watching her with that nibbling, needing look.

Janis was almost tempted to leave everything, she was so tired. She looked at her daughter.

'No,' she said aloud. 'We need to talk.'

'What about Alan?'

'Alan?'

'Yes, you remember. Alan, the . . . well, Alan.'

'What about him?'

'He's still here.'

He was still there. Everyone else had gone but he hadn't gone. He was still in the flat.

'Do you want me to ask him to leave?'

Violette moved away from her mother.

'It all depends on what you want to talk about,' she said now. 'It all depends on whether you want him with us whilst we're talking.'

Her mother frowned.

'Of course I don't want him with us. He usually sits in the kitchen and reads the paper or . . . or makes coffee or something.'

The girl wondered about the 'something'. What kind of something did Alan usually do?

'I'll tell him to go,' Janis put in now but Violette had changed her mind.

She couldn't bear the thought of Alan creeping back into the flat after she had finally left. If he crept back in, where did he creep to?

She shook her head. He wasn't like that. He wasn't,

was he?

'It doesn't matter. We can't have much left to say, anyway.'

Her mother was startled.

'Can't have much left to say?' she repeated. 'We haven't even started saying what needs to be said, Violette. We haven't even started.'

There was a heavy silence. Time was taking things up and away from them.

'Look, I'll tell him to go.'

Janis wasn't at all sleepy now.

'No. No, don't bother.'

Violette had thought Alan could go through her mother's door and she just might not see him again. Mother or no mother, she wanted, intended, to see him again and again.

'Come and sit by the fire.' Janis urged her forward. 'Sit there. Make yourself comfortable. Let's relax and talk.'

Then there was silence.

'So,' the girl broke it. 'You're still all together then, you and the . . . women.' She tried to remember names. 'You and Joan, and Anne and Sharon.' She couldn't remember any more. 'You're still together.'

Janis sighed.

'Yes, we're still together. They're my friends, Violette, that's all. Just my friends. Just women.'

'Oh yeah, your friends. Right.'

'So me and my friends are still together.'

Another silence.

'I'd have thought you'd have split up by now,' Violette returned. 'All this . . . erm, what did you call it? Oh yeah, individualism. You harped on about that, didn't you? About you all being individuals, flowering, all that. Yes, that's what you said. "She really flowered"' the girl quoted with bleak sarcasm.

Then she was quiet.

'There was a bit more to it than that.' Janis's voice was sharp and resentful. How had they got back on this old familiar road so fast?

'There was?' Violette pretended surprise. 'Oh. Well, what else was there, then?'

'My beliefs.' Her mother was rattled. 'My beliefs, Violette. Quaint as it may seem, I do have beliefs.'

'Then tell me what your beliefs are, mother. Go on, you just tell me. Convert me.'

Alan wandered in and out of the kitchen, in and out of the room. Violette saw he avoided the bedroom.

'I think I'll go now,' he said but neither of the two women wanted that.

Janis was quick to respond.

'Don't go, Alan. I was just going to make coffee. You've time for one last cup.'

She was obviously upset. Alan touched her face and smiled at her. Violette felt a surge of rage so fierce, she could have exploded.

'When you two have quite finished,' she said coldly. 'Perhaps you might give me an answer and stop avoiding the question, mother.'

She wanted a reply. She was determined to have one. 'Let me have it in the open,' the words banged in her head. 'Let me see what was so important you could just walk out and leave us to rot.'

'It sounded a stupid question to me,' Alan put in, sitting down.

His voice made Violette jump.

'It isn't stupid,' she retorted. 'And just because you say it is doesn't make it so.'

'It's stupid because if you haven't the wit to put all of it

124

together and add it up, then you don't deserve an answer. You don't even deserve a question.' He was angry with her. 'You know what it's all about, Violette, so don't try and kid us. You don't want to understand, that's your trouble. It's easier for you to keep saying it doesn't make sense.' Alan rattled the poker against the fire. 'It's easier to pull people down than to build them up.'

He flung the poker down and turned to her.

'Don't you tell me what's easy and what isn't,' Violette said furiously. 'It's easy for you all right because Janis isn't your mother but it isn't easy for me so just you keep your "easy" to yourself.'

'No,' Alan's voice was steady. 'No, she isn't my mother.'

Now, Janis put a hand on the young man's shoulder. She was pale.

'Not your mother,' Violette thought. 'But I bet she's something else.'

'You can be absolutely bloody at times, Violette, do you know that?'

Janis faced her.

'I mean, why? Why? What's it all for? All this hostility, all this hate. What's it in aid of?'

'It's not in aid of anything.' The girl jumped up and paced the room. Her mood changed. 'Oh, all right, I'm sorry.' She was flippant, uncaring. 'If you want an apology, there it is. I'm sorry. OK? I'm sorry.'

Her mother looked as if she was going to say more but stayed silent. Her head dropped and quite unexpectedly, Violette felt she loved her mother, loved her very much indeed. Sometimes when she felt like that, she got angry and resentful with Janis but not this time, now it softened her, made her want warm loving contact with her.

'Look, Mum,' she tried again. 'I'm honestly trying to understand. Honest I am.'

'Oh, Violette, Violette, Violette. I would have left, anyway. Your father and me, well, we'd come to the end of the road. It was time for one or the other of us to move on and you know your Dad, Violette, it would never have been him. Loyalty's written in him like words in a stick of rock. Someone had to do something. I didn't want my whole life, or your Dad's life, to be one of compromise. It was too much of a waste.'

Violette wondered how her mother could judge what was right for her father. She opened her mouth to deny every last word her mother had spoken but then she didn't. She realised she couldn't be bothered to deny something that might well be true, for all she knew. Whatever else her mother had taught her, she had taught her most of all that she knew nothing of the true reality of relationships.

After all, what about Alan? What about Alan?

Janis gave up. 'I'm going to make coffee.'

There was an air of defeat in the room. They all felt it. Violette thought now it would all have to wait. She could see the years pulling away from them in a welter of mistake and error. Somewhere in those years, she and Janis would have time, surely. They would have to make time.

The kitchen door clicked shut behind her mother. She glanced at Alan, wanting him to move across to her, wanting him to put his arms round her. She thought she could not spare her mother and then was shocked by the ease with which she gave her mother away.

'Once,' she started, watching Alan, 'my mother said she was a revolutionary. I laughed at her. So did my Dad.'

'That sounds par for the course.'

'Oh, stop that, Alan. Stop judging me all the time.'

Alan grinned.

'Yeah, yeah. You're right. OK. I'm sorry. Go on. What were you going to say?'

'Well, what I wanted to ask you was – is she a revolutionary? I mean, is that what she is?'

The young man shrugged.

'Oh, well, is she a revolutionary, are any of us revolutionaries?' He hesitated, unhappy with the word. 'I suppose. I suppose. You don't want to make too big a deal out of this, Violette. Janis found a cause; well, don't we all?'

He was tired.

'I haven't found a cause,' the girl protested.

'No.'

'So is she a revolutionary?' Violette persisted. 'I mean, what is a revolutionary – if she is one?'

She felt somewhere in the word lay the truth.

'Why don't you look it up?' Alan suggested but Violette didn't want to do that.

'You tell me,' she insisted. 'I want you to tell me.'

'Well, then, I guess you'd say a revolutionary is an instigator. An innovator. A creator of new conditions.' Alan looked impatient. 'Oh, hell, I don't know. What? What? One who brings about change.' A pause. 'Got that? A person who brings about change. OK?'

Violette nodded.

'Yeah,' she said. That was certainly what her mother had done.

There had to be other ways, didn't there?

'Does it always have to be violent change?'

Alan shrugged.

'You have to define your terms,' he said. 'You're not playing with the concept. You can play at being the word revolutionary but the reality of the word isn't open to play. When you look at it, Violette, any change from an existing state is, in a sense, a violent change. You should understand that.'

'Can't you have peaceful change?' she asked and he

laughed at her – 'You're so mournful,' – and laughed again. 'Stop wanting things your own way, my girl. If you cut your finger, you change the finger. Right?'

She bridled.

'I said I understood.'

'Well, there you are then. One cut finger.'

He reached over and picked up her hand, bent his head and kissed a finger. She couldn't cope with that and pulled her hand away.

'You're not taking me seriously.'

'I am.'

'Alan, you're not.'

He held his hands up.

'All right. Listen carefully. A revolutionary creates great and violent change for the common good.' He stopped.

She nodded.

'Right.'

'And give us a kiss,' he went on.

'What?'

'Give us a kiss.'

She rose to her feet and walked to the kitchen door. She pushed it open and when her mother turned, said, 'I'm going home. I'll see you tomorrow.'

Janis was surprised.

'But you haven't had your coffee.'

'I don't want any coffee.'

Her mother put the cups down.

'I'll come with you. It's too late for you to be out on your own.'

Violette didn't reply. She picked her coat up from the back of the sofa and went out. Alan didn't move and she was too fast for her mother. The door to the flat banged behind her and she ran down the stairs with hot, angry tears pouring down her face. What did he think she was?

An idiot?

At least, she thought bitterly, she hadn't cried in front of Janis again. There was that much to be thankful for.

By the time her mother caught her up, the tears were finished.

'Wait for me,' Janis called, breathless through running. 'Why do you have to be so . . . so . . .'

'Mum.' Violette whirled round. 'Do me a favour. Don't, just don't ask me why I'm this, that or the other. I don't need all this criticism and I don't want it.'

'Neither do I,' Janis retorted. 'Neither do I.'

They were facing each other.

'Just tell me one thing,' Violette said.

'What?'

'How did you get anyone to take *you* seriously?'

Janis frowned.

'Yes, well, that's a whole story to itself, Violette, and one I'm sure you could write.'

Violette grinned.

'All right?' her mother smiled.

'All right,' the girl echoed, stumbling over the words. 'OK, I take your point.'

They hugged.

'You were right,' Janis said, pulling away. 'We couldn't talk with Alan there. I wanted to tell you this – that I believed in the Miners' strike, that I still believe in it, that I would believe in it whenever, whatever. It's true about me and your father but even, even if we had been happy together, I would still have done exactly what I have done.' She paused and looked closely into Violette's face. 'It's important to me that you believe that.'

There was no sound anywhere.

'I did what I thought was the right thing to do,' Janis went on. 'And for me, it was the right thing. If I had one

129

wish for you, Violette, one wish for you as my daughter, as a woman, I wouldn't wish for happiness for you, or money or fame. What I would wish would be that you found yourself strong enough to do as I have done. The greatest happiness in this world is to stand up for what you believe in. That's what I wish for you. Courage – the courage to fight for what you believe in.'

They linked arms for the rest of the short way home, Violette became aware of a loved and familiar scent.

'Where's your new perfume?' she asked. 'That Indian stuff?'

'Oh, that,' her mother smiled. 'I couldn't get used to it so I've gone back to my old sort.'

'Mum.'

The girl stopped but her mother touched her face. 'Go on,' she said. 'You call me whatever you want. It's like the perfume. I got carried away.' She grinned. 'I threw the baby out with the bathwater.'

They both laughed. Then, the house was in front of them.

'Mum,' she started again. 'Janis –' Then, more strongly, 'Janis, are you having an affair with Alan?'

'That's none of your business,' a voice broke in and Violette turned to see Alan standing behind her. Again, he'd been there and she hadn't been aware of him.

She bowed her head.

'No,' she said. 'I don't suppose it is,' and left them both.

They were still there as she closed the door behind her.

Chapter Eleven

A day passed. Violette made no effort to do her schoolwork. She made no effort to go to school, drifting round the house bored and unhappy.

Her Dad grumbled at her.

'That school'll be on my back again. You never do any studying at all. They said you wouldn't pass one exam at the rate you're going. Not one.' He rubbed a hand across his face. 'I'm worried about you. It's been a long time now. You can't keep blaming us for everything. You should go to school. You should do your homework.'

She made no reply.

She could pass an exam all right, she thought with bitterness. She could answer any questions on . . . on love, *luv, lurve* . . . on her mother and Alan . . . On how it hurt to know he was having an affair with Janis. On how when she thought of her mother, she thought of her mother's lips being touched by his lips. She moved restlessly, breathless with pain.

Her father walked across the room and sat on the arm of her chair.

'Now look, love,' he started. 'Your brother's adjusting, so . . .'

She exploded. This was what she needed.

'Mark's adjusting? Is that what you said? Mark's

131

adjusting.' She laughed. 'Oh yes, he's adjusting all right. You just ask him where he spends every night. Go on, just ask him. Let's see how Mark's adjusting.'

Her Dad's face went sharp.

'Why, where does he spend every night?'

'Don't ask me. I'm not your spy. If you want to know, ask him.'

'Mark tells me he's going to his pals.'

'Oh well, if that's what Mark tells you.'

'Are you saying he doesn't?'

'Ask him and see.'

'I'm asking you. You're the one who says he's lying. Is he lying?'

'Well, he doesn't go to any pals, I can tell you that. If you must know, he goes to the Amusement Arcade and he's mixing with lads from school who're always in trouble. That's how Mark's adjusting. You and Janis, you don't care what happens as long as you don't see it happening.'

Her father stood up.

'I'm going to ignore that because I'm sick and tired of that kind of crack.'

'Ignore it then.'

He took a deep breath.

'I shall have a word with Mark when he comes in.'

'Oh yes, tell him I split on him. I shall be popular.'

'You needn't worry,' her Dad said shortly. 'I shan't bring you into anything.'

They seemed held in the room, in the thick miserable silence they had created. Violette didn't know how to break it. She stared at her Dad and was struck by how much he'd changed.

Janis had gone into browns and greys, blacks and purples, as if a light, bright colour would offend her. Now, Violette could see her Dad had got sharper and sharper, even at the weekends. He wore suits all the time. She couldn't remember now when she had last seen him in jeans and sweatshirt. When he wanted to relax, he opened the top button of his shirt and loosened his tie. That was as far as he ever went.

'Why are you always dressed up?' she asked but he turned a weary face to her.

'Why don't you try and think things through for yourself?'

Her father moved to her and peered in her face.

'What's this then? Tears? Come on, V. You're a big girl now. Don't let's have any more tears. For God's sake, no more tears.'

Clumsily, he dabbed at her eyes. She knocked his arm away.

'Don't worry, there won't be any tears from me. I've done all the crying I'm going to do.'

Her father put his arms round her, just as he used to when she was little. Violette stiffened and pulled back.

'Come on, kid,' her Dad pleaded.

She relaxed enough to give him a quick hug and with a rueful smile, he let her go.

'Dad, you've been telling me to grow up. Well, now I have.'

'So you don't want any more hugs?'

An unexpected lightness came into the room as she hesitated between shaking and nodding her head.

'Go on,' he teased. 'It's nice to have a hug.'

He held his arms out to her and, smiling reluctantly, she moved into them. Her Dad grinned down at her. All the tears were gone. A warmth of feeling was in the air and for the first time in a long time, they were together without bitterness.

Violette's father danced her round the room and as they

twirled past the door, it opened and Mark stepped in. He stopped short when he saw them.

'What's the matter with you two?' he asked.

His Dad let go of Violette.

'Oh,' he smiled. 'Just practising our dancing steps.'

Mark grunted.

Violette saw her father chew his bottom lip, his face set now and thoughtful.

'You're just the lad I want to see,' he started but Mark tensed with suspicion.

'What do you want to see me for?'

'I wondered if you'd help me with your Granny's decorating tonight?'

Mark pondered this.

'I can't,' he said at last. 'I'm going out.'

Peter's face hardened.

'Oh. I see.'

Mark turned to his sister.

'Anything for tea?'

'There's some frozen pies and oven-ready chips. I'm going to heat them through in a minute.'

Her brother groaned.

'Why can't we ever have proper food? I'm sick of frozen chips and pies.'

'You cook it, you can have it,' Violette retorted. 'I'm not cooking all the time. No wonder I never get any homework done.'

Their father lifted his hands.

'Hold it. Hold it. No more arguing. I'll tell you what we're going to do. We're going out for a good meal. There's going to be some changes round here.'

'I can't go. I've told you – I'm going out with Mum.'

'What time are you meeting her?' his Dad asked, hiding his surprise.

'Nine.'

'That's a bit late, isn't it? You've got school tomorrow.'

'Mum said you wouldn't mind. We're going to watch a video.'

'I don't mind,' Peter emphasised. 'It's just that it's a bit late when you have to go to school. OK. OK.' He held up a hand. 'This once but, Mark, not as late in future if it's school the next day. Anyway, surely there's time for you to come for a meal with us.'

Mark grudgingly agreed there would be time and Violette felt a surge of happiness.

She grinned at her brother.

'Come on, then. Let's hurry up before he changes his mind.'

For a little while, at least, a lightness was in the house and, standing outside her bedroom door, she hoped against hope that it would last.

She was not going to think about Alan and Janis. That could wait. She shivered. She pushed open the door and grabbed her coat. Time enough to worry when it happened.

It was later that she saw the grey man again. They had eaten their meal and Violette had offered to buy the coffees. Her father had accepted and she scrabbled in her bag for the money, head bent as she searched the deeper recesses of her shoulder bag.

She was flushed with laughing. It had been such a good evening. It hadn't been the same as when her mother had been with them but just for a little while, she had felt part of a real family once more. Part of a group of people who cared for each other.

At last she found her purse. It was as she looked up into the restaurant that she saw him through the far window. The lace curtains hanging from the polished wood were caught back in the middle and just for a second, he stood there.

She felt a quick pang of fear. Who was he? What did he want? Was he following *her* now and if he was, why?

Alan's words echoed in her head. 'Special Branch'. Really? Really the Special Branch? No. No, it couldn't be. Yet, she wondered. Did he think Alan was with her?

Alan. Alan. Alan.

She felt cold and her hand shook as she handed her Dad the money for the coffee.

He glanced at her, concerned.

'Something wrong?' he asked but she shook her head.

'No. No, there's nothing wrong. It's been a lovely night, Dad.'

They were all more subdued when they left the restaurant. Violette scoured the high street but there was no sign now of the grey man. Again she wondered if she was imagining things.

'Looking for someone?' Her Dad was casual.

'No, I'm not looking for anyone.'

Mark was impatient to be gone and although he nodded when his father told him to be careful, not to be in too late and all the other automatic warnings, he clearly had left them already in spirit.

'Look, I'll walk you home and then I'm going for a pint.' Peter said, watching Mark hurry down the road.

'You don't have to walk me home. I'm quite capable of getting home on my own.'

Her Dad hesitated, torn between wanting to be gone and yet wanting the early promise of the evening to be fulfilled.

'If you're sure?'

'Of course I'm sure.'

Peter gave her a last smile and then he was gone, too.

Violette looked after him. In front of her father, she could still see Mark. She felt as if all her life had now been reduced to watching people leave and she marvelled that it hadn't happened before. That she hadn't been aware of how insubstantial and frail the ties were that bound one to one. Cobwebs.

She took a deep breath. This was the other thing. She glanced up and down the street. She was always on her own since Janis had left. No-one seemed to much want to be with her in that exclusive way her mother had.

She made a slight clicking noise with her tongue. That was the trouble, wasn't it? Her mother hadn't wanted to be with her – in any way, exclusive or otherwise.

Yet, last night . . . She paused. Janis had wanted her to . . . wanted her to spend time with her. That was last night. Was there really any new ground between her and her mother? She thought of Alan. The only new ground was a swamp.

And through it all, she wished Alan was with her. Now. That was what she really wanted, for Alan to appear out of a doorway, round a corner, anywhere, just so long as he was there. Just so long as he was hers and not her mother's.

Violette wandered down the street. The traffic lights at the bottom showed red. She saw her Dad cross the road in front of the lights, saw him go into the pub.

Thinking of Alan, she thought of desire.

'Then desire me when thou wilt, if ever now.'

She stopped.

That wasn't ' . . . desire me . . .', that was 'Then hate me when thou wilt, if ever now.'

Desire.

She became aware of her own body. Of the light tickling of her tongue on the inside of her lips. Of the warm smoothness of her skin. She wondered if you could feel desire for yourself.

No. It was Alan's tongue. Alan's skin. Alan's body. It was him. She wanted him to the point where it hurt not having him. She wanted him by her side, wanted his hand in hers but he wasn't there. He never would be there.

A breeze ruffled her hair and cooled her cheeks.

'Oh, well,' she sighed aloud, moving through the dusty town.

She drifted down the garden path towards the house. It was all too late. Nothing could happen now. She turned her key in the lock, opened the door and stepped into the hall.

The light from the street lamps shone along the walls and floor. She stood there, in the darkness, and looked around. She loved the shadows and the movement of light. Tonight she was full of love. She loved the smooth fall of the banister. She moved to the stairs and bent her hot cheek against the cool wood. It felt like Alan's hand. It melted into her skin, the coolness, the hard strength of the wood.

By the time she reached her room, she was exhausted. She felt dizzy with need. She wanted . . . she wanted and yet, she scarcely knew what it was she did want.

She put a record on and undressed slowly to the music. She swayed into bed and switched out the light, closing her eyes, expecting sleep to come easily.

An hour later, she sat up. The bed was hateful to her. The covers made her sweat. The pillows were rocks, making her head and neck ache until she felt sick with it.

She got up and stood against the window, looking into the street.

Where was Alan? Where was he?

Chapter Twelve

Friday was a day of sunshine and showers. Tired and headachy, Violet almost decided not to go to school. School was beginning to seem so irrelevant, she could barely focus on it.

'Exams,' Mr Davies commented. 'You know, Violette, those things you have to study for?'

Violette indicated she knew what exams were.

'Oh,' Mr Davies said. 'Good Lord, you do surprise me. I mean, are the Examiners going to be treated to the same level of intellectual rigour evident in your last Shakespeare paper?'

Violette would have given a lot for the teacher to have vanished in a puff of smoke. She glared at him but this cut less ice than she'd hoped.

'Don't glower at me, Miss,' Mr Davies went on unforgivingly. 'If you could bear to turn your thoughts to this new essay?' He held up a book. 'The one that concentrates on this book, for instance.'

Violette stared at the book. She had never even heard of it. Or had she? With a sinking heart, she remembered it was on her Reading List.

'Yes,' Mr Davies carried on smoothly, correctly interpreting her look of sick dismay. 'You've heard of it, you may even have been in class when we were reading it but – and here is the sixty-four thousand dollar question – did you take any of it in?'

This time he didn't wait for an answer but turned away from her with impatience.

The morning seemed endless. At lunch break, Violette carried out of the classroom the book Mr Davies had held up. She must try and read it. She sat in the quietest corner of the Library. There was such a lot to think about but every time she tried to sort things out in her head, she started a ferocious headache.

She opened the book. The first paragraph was promising.

Mr Davies stood and watched her. He pursed his lips together. What could he do to help the girl, he wondered. He'd seen her take the book from the classroom. Here she was in the Library. He'd watched her open it and that was that. Nothing. She would fail her exams and he was sorry about this because of the promise she had in her.

Parents, he thought savagely. What selfish devils they were. Why couldn't they choose the proper time to leave if they had to leave? He wondered how many young lives had been blighted by parents taking off before exams. Selfish devils, he repeated. It was all right for them, they'd had their chance but the kids . . . . He shrugged and decided to make one more attempt.

He walked across to Violette and asked if he could join her.

The girl glanced up at him and nodded. He was almost sure she had very little idea of who he was and what he was doing there. She seemed unfocused and vague.

'Interesting?' He indicated the book.

'Oh. Oh yes, very interesting,' Violette came to earth with a thump.

She looked with dismay at the book. Glory, she hadn't

read a word past the first paragraph. She felt overwhelmed with despair. It was crumbling around her. Her whole world, even worse now than before. Before when? She couldn't be sure. Before the Strike or before Alan or before Alan and her mother together? Who knew?

She could hear Mr Davies talking, see his lips moving but she couldn't make sense of the words.

'Violette –' Mr Davies touched her arm. 'Violette,' he said, louder. 'You must study. The exams . . .' he stopped. What was the point? 'If you do a crash study, you might still stand a chance but you'd have to start now.' He emphasised this. 'Now, Violette, do you understand?'

And suddenly she did understand. The exams were important to her. Alan was important to her. But she wanted to pass her exams. Yes, she did. So much had been taken away from her, she didn't want that taken away as well. She didn't want to fail by default as she seemed to have failed so often recently. If she was going to fail, then she wanted to fail properly.

She stared at Mr Davies and there was so much pain and distress on her face that the teacher wished he could do more for her.

'I'll give you the list of English books,' he said now. 'Because I don't believe you've got them.'

Violette could barely remember where her school bag was, let alone her books.

'Thank you,' she murmured. 'Thank you.'

It would be something to do. Now that was the idea which crept into her mind. It would fill in those long blank spaces of time.

Now she recollected her father saying, 'If you're not studying, it's because you don't want to.'

She wondered how fair that was but threw the thought out as quickly as it had come. There was nothing fair in the world. Fairness indicated a game with rules but she knew now that life wasn't like that. There were no rules because it wasn't a game, so 'fairness' or 'unfairness' didn't come into it.

She took the list of books from Mr Davies, picked up her novel and wandered out.

The teacher watched her go, then turned away. There was only so much you could do. After that, it was up to them.

Violette was going to cut the rest of the day. She couldn't concentrate so what was the point in going into class? Then she decided after all to go to the next lesson.

She trailed through the school, down the long corridors which smelt of bodies, until she turned into the bleak mess which was her classroom. The chairs and tables were tumbled about the scuffed floor.

One or two of her old friends tried to speak but she only nodded and went to sit at the back.

Rachel Benton stepped through the door.

'Heyup,' she said as she saw Violette. 'We've got Vi-o-let-tah with us today, have we?' She made a mock curtsey. 'And to what do we owe this honour?'

Violette stared through her.

'Stuck-up,' Benton said. 'You don't half think you're it, you do.'

There was an uneasiness in the room. Rachel felt it, too. She was half-hearted about her tauntings. There wasn't quite the support she had looked for.

'Why don't you shut up, Benton?' a voice cried and Rachel decided this wasn't the time or place to get her own back on Violette Saunders. And then she looked out of the window.

''Ere,' she crowed. 'There's your Mum's fancy man.'

She turned to Violet with a look of triumph.

'Well, what do you know about that? And 'e's here.' She whirled round, her skirts flying. 'Your Mum been lying about her age, then?'

There was a ripple of laughter in the room but Rachel wasn't interested. 'I fancy this one,' she said. She turned back to the window for a last look, then hurried out.

Violette kept her eyes to the front of the class. She didn't want to see Alan. She didn't believe he was there but even if he was, she still didn't want to see him.

Rachel's friends crowded to the windows.

'Here, look, cheeky thing. She's making up to him.'

'She'll be on his knee in a minute.'

'How can she get on his knee when he's standing up?'

'He's not going to be standing up long, is he, not at this rate,' another voice chipped in and the girls sniggered.

Violette stood up. She gazed out of the window. Yes, Rachel was there and yes, Alan was there too. The young man was stepping back from Rachel, but the girl was making him smile. He was grinning down at her, amused by her cockiness.

'You want to watch her, Saunders,' one of the girls warned. 'She's a dab hand at pinching other girl's fellas.'

Violette said nothing. She didn't know what to do. He wasn't her fellow and yet everything in her said he was. But she would not haggle over Alan as if he were an item on a market stall. He and she both deserved more dignity than that. If Benton wanted Alan and Alan wanted Benton, then they must do as they pleased.

'Whayhaaaay,' the crowd chanted. 'She's got his arm round her now.'

Violette watched steadily. Yes, she had. She had her hand in his and even as the girl watched, she saw Benton guide Alan's hand to the warm firm place under her breast.

Alan pulled his hand away as if it had been burnt. He

143

strode out towards the school.

'He's coming up here. Look, he's actually coming up here. Can you credit it!'

The girls cheered and giggled, yelling and waving as Alan and Rachel Benton drew closer to the main entrance.

Alan glanced over. He stopped abruptly when he saw the girls at the window, running his eyes over them. When his face quickened, Violette knew he had seen her.

The young man pushed the importuning Rachel to one side. Now he knew where he was going and he ran through the school doors, allowing them to swing back at the girl.

'Violette. Violette. Where are you?'

Everyone could hear him. The room fell silent and as the next teacher walked in, Violette thought only of getting to Alan's side.

Again the roar.

'Violette. Violette. You come out here. Come on. I want you.'

He was going to get her into trouble. Violette moved swiftly, hurrying past the startled teacher. She sped down the hall and just as Alan opened his mouth to shout again, she called to him, 'Alan. Be quiet. I'm here.'

The receptionist slammed the glass door of the partition back into place, glaring at them from her office.

'Be quiet. We'll both get into bother.'

He looked at her and grinned.

'Now then,' he said slowly and the smile spread over his words like honey. 'Now then, Violette. You're coming with me. We've a lot to talk about.'

She smiled back. She couldn't help but smile back. Her smile felt so wide and full of energy. It was for him. Everything else was quite forgotten.

Then they were outside, out in the wide sunlit grounds.

Mr Davies hurried towards them. He stopped in front

of Violette.

'Take these books. I've got them together for you. Now, remember what I said. You're still in with a chance if you get down to some studying.'

Violette took the books. 'Yes,' she said. 'I've got a lot of work to do.'

Mr Davies stood back as the two walked away.

'Hmm,' he murmured. 'Let's hope he's got more sense than her parents.'

Outside the school, walking down the green shadowed road to town, Alan told her, 'There's no affair. Never has been. It isn't that sort of relationship. Sure, I like your Mum. Who wouldn't? But that's all, Violette. We see each other because we're involved in the same concerns. It's you.' He turned her to him. 'It's you, Violette.'

He kissed her, holding her gently at first and then as the kiss went on, his arms grew harder, binding her to him.

When they drew apart, Violette thought she would never be so happy again.

'I . . .' she looked up at him and her lips kept on with the crazy need to smile. 'I think I . . .'

He put a finger over her lips. For a moment, a piercing memory came back of the night she was attacked. She pulled his hand away and stepped back.

Before she could explain, before she could say anything, his attention was drawn to the road.

A police car cruised past, followed by one of the big dark anonymous vans the police were now using all the time. The van pulled into the side of the road just beyond them and Alan turned to face it.

He stood, silent and watchful, as the grey man got out and walked towards them.

Violette grew wary. She moved closer to Alan. The man stopped in front of them.

'Your card's marked, my lad.' He looked at Violette. 'And you, the actress's daughter –' he paused. 'You be very careful.'

He said no more but walked steadily back to the van. Its sides had been caged with black steel grids. It had started up and was moving before the door slammed behind him.

'He scares me,' Violette whispered. 'Really scares me.'

'Yeah.'

They were quiet, standing together.

'What I came to tell you,' Alan began, 'was that I'm going to a big meeting at Surrey Main.'

'When?' She was afraid for him.

'Now.' He leant forward as he spoke, his face stern. 'I'm getting a lift. In a minute.' He stroked her hair, cupping her chin in his hand, then drawing a finger over her lips. 'I've got a feeling it's my turn today. That's why I wanted to see you. To sort things out. I don't want there to be any misunderstanding between us. I want you to be my girl.' He paused. 'Will you?'

She nodded. 'You know I will.'

'Yes,' he grinned, then grew serious again. 'It's just that there might not be a lot of time left. In the immediate future, that is. These days anything can happen. I might vanish for a couple of months. Be put away.'

'Yes.'

'That's how it is,' he was insistent. 'It's best for you to know that. I don't even know how things'll turn out today, but I have to go. I'm a Union man. You stand up for what you believe in, no question.' He was adamant. 'No question. It isn't always possible to be on the same side, not even with them you think a lot of. Not when it's a question of beliefs.'

Violette took his hand.

'I know all about that,' she said.

For the first time in her life she thought of her namesake, Violette Szabo. She was glad she had that girl's name. She wondered what Violette Szabo would have made of it all.

'All the same, I wish more than anything in the world you didn't have to go.'

'Yeah. Well.' The young man stopped. 'That's how it is, Violette.'

With great certainty, Violette pulled him to her, her authority the tenderness that engulfed her.

'Alan,' she said. 'Watch out. Be careful.'

Gently, Alan released himself and smiled down at her.

'Don't worry, I'll watch out all right – and I'll be back. Count on it, Violette.'

They stood together, yet already apart, each in a separate demanding world.

Then a car drew up and the young men inside it took Alan away from her by their presence and their joking words.

Before she could properly take it in, he had gone and not a quarter of all the things they needed to say had been said.

She stared after the car.

'Be careful,' she whispered. 'Watch what you're doing.'

There was no way to go then but home.

Chapter Thirteen

The first thing Violette did when she got in was to sort out the books Mr Davies had given her. They had been heavy to carry. Alan had almost forgotten to hand them to her, sprinting back at the last minute and pushing them into her arms.

Now, she turned them over and inspected the covers as if they were written in some strange and exotic language. The very words jumped about. At last she had them sorted. Novels, poetry, odds and ends. Yes. She fingered one pile, then another.

What she intended to do was to make out a study chart. She intended to draw blue lines on white paper and fill in squares of time with the title of each book. She could see it in her head. She could account for all the reading she would need to do before the exams.

When, after an hour, she realised she had done nothing further but stare at the books, she went to make a cup of coffee. Passing the telephone in the hall, she dialled her mother's number then put the receiver down before it could ring.

'This is no good,' she said aloud.

Nothing happened. The words disappeared.

Where was Alan? That was the only pressing need she felt. Where was Alan? She thought of the clear steady face marked with blood then impatiently shook the image away.

There was no need for melodrama.

In and out of the room, up and down the stairs to her bedroom, touching the telephone, picking it up, putting it down.

'Stop it,' she shouted at last. 'Just stop it.'

Violette seized a book, opening it at random, trying to read. Hopeless. She flung the book on to the sofa.

Her eyes felt tired and at last, she dragged herself to her bed and lay down. She was quiet, thinking she wouldn't sleep. How could she sleep with the memory of the grey man, with the thought of Alan in her head? But she did sleep and didn't waken until the sound of the telephone shrilled through the house.

She was surprised when the ringing cut off and, getting to her feet, opened her door and stepped into the hall.

'Is anybody there?' she called down the stairs. She glanced at her watch. It was mid-afternoon. No-one else should be in the house. Had she locked the door when she'd come in? She couldn't remember.

She walked to the top of the stairs.

'Is anybody there?' Her voice louder.

Then she heard someone speaking. With a shock of relief she recognised the voice.

'Dad,' she shouted to him, running down the stairs. 'Dad.' She was glad he was home. She needed to talk to him.

He turned slowly from the telephone, his face white with worry.

'It's your mother,' he said. 'She's been arrested.'

Violette felt as if someone had kicked her in the stomach. Janis couldn't have been arrested. How did you get arrested?

'She's what?'

'She's been arrested. You can hear what I'm saying.' He was anxious now, moving quickly about the hall.

'But how, why, where?'

Her Dad sighed, pulling his coat on, checking his wallet for money.

'She was on some sort of picket line again. I don't know. A mass demonstration or something. At Surrey Main. You know what they're up to, mass meetings, picket lines, demonstrations.' He rubbed a hand over his face. 'Why? That's what I want to know. Why? I ask myself a thousand times a day.'

He stopped, as if becoming aware once more of his daughter.

'Hmm. Well, you know what it's like, Violette. You've seen them. It was bound to happen sometime. The woman who's just phoned said your Mum had been marked out.' He scratched his head. 'Marked out. I don't know. They say things . . . well, you have to take them with a pinch of salt but I . . .' He stopped again, then went on hopelessly, 'I don't know.'

Marked out. Marked out. Violette could hear the grey man. Those were his words but wasn't there some confusion here? He'd meant them for Alan. 'You've been marked out.' No, she turned from her father. 'Your card's marked.' That was it. It wasn't only Alan's card that had been marked, then, but Janis's as well.

She sat down on the bottom step of the staircase. They were both involved in this. She could lose them both.

Her father was talking again.

'They said she was picked out for special treatment. They were watching for her. They knew she'd be there.'

'How did they know?'

He lifted his hands.

'Spies, I suppose. That's how all these things are run,

isn't it?'

They looked at each other, a weary puzzlement on both their faces.

'Yes,' Violette agreed. 'Yes, that's the way they're run.'

There was a short silence as her father hurried through to the room. When he came back, he was ready to leave.

'Where are you going?'

'I'm going for your mother.'

'Can I come?'

He nodded.

'I wouldn't try to stop you.'

The Police Station was several miles away. On the road out, they stopped and waited for Mark to come out of school. He clambered into the car with them, all astonishment and questions. As soon as he knew where they were going, his lips tightened and his face grew somehow younger. Watching him, Violette was reminded of the photographs of him as a baby.

'She'll be all right, Mark. You'll see. Dad'll get her back.'

The boy stared wordlessly through the car window.

On the drive, Peter went obsessively over and over the information he'd had.

'They strip search them.'

Violette turned her head and stared at him in blank astonishment.

'They what?'

'They strip search them.'

'They strip search them?'

'That's what they told me. Is it true? Do you know if it's true?'

They stopped for traffic lights. He drummed his fingers on the steering wheel.

'Dad, I don't know if it's true. I don't know what to

151

believe any more at all.'

Mark burrowed further down into his jacket. His face was set and closed.

Violette thought of her mother being strip searched. Her own body flushed at the thought of it.

They were a silent, unhappy party who finally reached the Police Station. They had considerable trouble being seen to at all. There were people everywhere. Finally, Peter managed to state his business and they were asked to wait.

Violette sat and watched. She was deeply unhappy.

She could hardly believe now that there had been a time when she had not been concerned about politics. She hadn't even seen the miners' strike as political. Was it or wasn't it? All she knew was that if the strike was the fruit of all political thought and endeavour out of the last hundreds of years, no wonder there were wars and revolutions. She felt a four-year-old with a meccano set could have done better.

Now, she looked at the swing doors opening and closing and thought it seemed as if every single thing was political. The leaves on the trees, the moon in the sky, the functions of the body, all, political.

They waited and waited. Mark hunched up and refused to be part of any of the experience. He wouldn't move or speak. He wouldn't pull his long legs in to allow others to pass by him. He simply sat and waited.

It was many hours before Janis was finally released and when she did come into the bleak little area, her face was strained.

'Let's go,' she said stiffly.

That was their only greeting.

Peter wanted to put his arms round her but she suffered his comfort for only a minute or two before pulling away.

They had a happier drive back. Janis sat in the back with Mark. The two of them talked incessantly, the words now sharp, now soft, until they reached the town.

Janis wanted to go to her flat but neither her husband or daughter would have this, he lifting his hand as if to ward off her words, Violette saying firmly, 'You're coming home,' until, in the end, Janis gave in and they went back to the family house.

They made coffee strong enough to melt teaspoons. Janis went straight to the bathroom and ran a bath so hot, Violette thought her mother's skin would peel off.

'You can't get in there,' she said but Janis stripped and almost plunged into the burning healing water.

She told Violette what happened to women when they were strip searched and in response, the girl fetched every kind of bath salt she could find. She poured the sweet scented salts into the water until her mother stopped her.

'I'm OK. Really. It doesn't matter any more, Violette.' She paused. 'We all knew what the penalty could be and we were all prepared for it to happen.'

Violette didn't believe a word of this. Knowing was one thing but, as she'd found, experience was quite another.

'Yeah,' she said.

'We've come a long way, Violette.' Her mother's voice was soft and thoughtful.

'Was it worth it?' Violette asked now, watching her mother soap her body.

Her mother nodded.

'Yes,' she said. 'It must always be worth it.'

There was silence again until Peter knocked on the door and shoved a strong drink round for his wife.

'Give her this,' he said and Violette took it to her mother.

'I wanted to ask you,' she said, handing her the drink,

153

trying to stop her hand shaking. 'Did you see anything of Alan? Do you know where he is?'

Janis shook her head.

'I'm sorry, love. I know he was there because I saw him but after I was arrested, they sat me in a van with a policewoman and I couldn't see anything else at all.'

Violette found the heat of the bathroom oppressive.

'I'm going down. It's too hot in here.'

'Listen,' Janis stopped her. 'Why don't you go and see his mother? Ask her if she's heard anything.'

His mother. She had never thought about his mother, not once. She hadn't even known if he had a mother, if he had a father, brothers, sisters.

'Do you think I should?'

Janis was feeling better. The bath, the drink had helped.

'Ye-es' she murmured. 'Yes, you go and see his mother. She'll know.'

There was a rap on the door.

'You all right in there?' Peter's voice was dry and non-committal.

Janis sighed and then looked at Violette.

'Tell your Dad we're all right.'

'No, I'm not going to do that,' Violette responded. 'You tell him. It's down to you. I'm going to find out about Alan.' She half turned then stopped. 'Do you remember the grey man?'

Janis nodded.

'Yes.'

'He spoke to me today.'

Her mother looked at her in surprise.

'He called me "the actress's daughter".' The girl traced a rivulet of moisture down the tiled wall.

Her mother waited.

'I'd correct him if he said it to me now. I'd say "I'm not

the actress's daughter. I'm the Revolutionary's daughter.'"

They smiled at each other, these two friends, mother and daughter. Then, as Violette's father knocked again, the girl left.

'Your mother all right?' her Dad asked. Then Janis was shouting, 'Come on in, Peter. Just come on in.'

He touched her shoulder then stepped into the bathroom.

Violette walked slowly down the stairs. She was beginning to understand. The answer to her question 'What is a Revolutionary?' was not simply the dry bones of Alan's reply. Words were elastic and their meanings multiple. The answer to any question depended on where you were standing politically when it was asked and when it was answered.

Mark was standing in the hall. He looked up at his sister.

'How long's Mum gonna be?'

Violette shrugged.

'She's getting a bath.'

'She's been in hours,' the boy complained. 'And there's never anything to eat in this house.'

'Why don't you go and get something to eat yourself?' Violette could hardly believe her brother hadn't changed. 'Everybody else,' she said tersely, 'reacts to change. Not you. You're like a human dustbin wandering around asking for food all the time. You'd think you couldn't boil an egg.'

'Oh, shut up,' Mark grumbled. 'I've only got to open my mouth round here and I get a lecture.'

Violette started to laugh.

'You're terrible, Mark,' she said.

The laughter finished as suddenly as it had started.

'Well, when's she coming down?' the boy persisted.

Violette shook her head.

'I don't know.'

'Is she stopping with us now, then? I mean, for keeps.'

'I shouldn't think so, Mark. Well, not straight away, anyway.'

Mark fell into step beside her as Violette went to fetch her coat.

'Where are you going?'

'I'm going to find out what's happened to Alan.'

'Why, have they let him go?'

Violette froze.

'Have who let him go?'

'Didn't I tell you?' Mark said. 'I saw him at the Police Station. He was with a load of other youths. They were taking them round the back.'

Violette sat down. She had no strength left.

'Why didn't you tell me?' she asked. 'Oh Mark, why didn't you tell me? I could have gone to him. I could have . . .'

'You couldn't have done anything. There were people everywhere. You'd only have shown him up. That's why I didn't tell you. He didn't want you chucking your arms round him and crying all over the place.'

She bent her head down. She felt so faint. So, he'd gone then. She wondered when she would see him again. If he was away a long time, would he remember her? Would he still feel the same way?

She lifted her head wearily and rose to her feet.

'Tell Dad I won't be long.'

The night was cool and bright. The moon was riding high again.

She paused at the gate and turned to look at the house. There would be a square of light at the side where her mother and father were together. The front was dark and quiet.

She turned and looked up the street. If her Dad knew

what she was doing, he'd stop her. The thought propelled her forward.

Where was Alan? Where was he? In the middle of her longing, she could still wish for the old sweet days of innocence. The innocence of not knowing.

Then she heard a shout.

'Violette.'

Her Dad.

'Violette!'

It was more imperative.

That wasn't her Dad. She looked up and he was there, walking towards her. She sat on the low garden wall and waited for him. The brick was warm from the long golden day.

He stopped in front of her.

'Whose are the roses?' he asked, grinning.

She glanced at the roses pushing their creamy heads through the black iron railings.

'They're my Dad's.'

He grinned again.

'Then they'll have to do,' and reaching over, he snapped a rose free and handed it to her.

Violette took the flower and as she did so, a thorn pierced her skin.

'Ouch!' She almost let the rose drop.

At once he was serious and concerned. He took the flower back and turned her hand over, so that he could examine her finger.

'It's made it bleed.'

'Only a drop.'

She dismissed the blood.

He lifted her hand to his lips and kissed her palm. His eyes caught with hers and their faces grew intent and preoccupied.

'They didn't mark your card, then?' she whispered, watching the lips buried in her hand.

He raised his head.

'No,' he grinned, and she smiled back. Here it was again, that same sparky joy in each other.

'Oh, Glory!' Violette thought.

'No,' he repeated and they were almost laughing. 'This time they only pencilled in my name.'

A selected list of title available from Teens · Mandarin

While every effort is made to keep prices low, it is sometimes necessary to increase prices at short notice. Mandarin Paperbacks reserves the right to show new retail prices on covers which may differ from those previously advertised in the text or elsewhere.

The prices shown below were correct at the time of going to press.

☐	7497 0009 2	**The Secret Diary of Adrian Mole Aged 13¾**	Sue Townsend	£2.50
☐	7497 0101 3	**The Growing Pains of Adrian Mole**	Sue Townsend	£2.50
☐	7497 0018 1	**Behind the Bike Sheds**	Jan Needle	£2.25
☐	416 10352 9	**Lexie**	Mary Hooper	£1.99
☐	416 08282 3	**After Thursday**	Jean Ure	£1.99
☐	416 10192 5	**A Tale of Time City**	Diana Wynne-Jones	£1.99
☐	416 07442 1	**Howl's Moving Castle**	Diana Wynne-Jones	£1.95
☐	416 08822 8	**The Changeover**	Margaret Mahy	£1.95
☐	416 13102 6	**Frankie's Story**	Catherine Sefton	£1.99
☐	416 11962 X	**Teens Book of Love Stories**	Miriam Hodgeson	£1.95
☐	416 12022 9	**Picture Me Falling In Love**	June Foley	£1.99
☐	416 12612 X	**All the Fun of the Fair**	Anthony Masters	£2.25
☐	416 13862 4	**Rough Mix**	Denis Bond	£1.99
☐	416 08082 0	**Teenagers Handbook**	Murphy/Grime	£1.99

All these books are available at your bookshop or newsagent, or can be ordered direct from the publisher. Just tick the titles you want and fill in the form below.

Mandarin Paperbacks, Cash Sales Department, PO Box 11, Falmouth, Cornwall TR10 9EN.

Please send cheque or postal order, no currency, for purchase price quoted and allow the following for postage and packing:

UK   80p for the first book, 20p for each additional book ordered to a maximum charge of £2.00.

BFPO   80p for the first book, 20p for each additional book.

Overseas   £1.50 for the first book, £1.00 for the second and 30p for each additional book
including Eire thereafter.

NAME (Block letters) ....

ADDRESS ....

....

....